THE MAGIC AQUIFER

Treating the Political Stress Syndrome

A Novel by
John R. Krismer, MHA-LFACHE

CCB Publishing
British Columbia, Canada

The Magic Aquifer:
Treating the Political Stress Syndrome, A Novel

Copyright ©2012 by John R. Krismer
ISBN-13 978-1-77143-010-4
First Edition

Library and Archives Canada Cataloguing in Publication
Krismer, John R., 1927-
The magic aquifer : treating the political stress syndrome,
a novel / written by John R. Krismer – 1st ed.
ISBN 978-1-77143-010-4
Additional cataloguing data available from Library and Archives Canada

Cover artwork: Northern Lights image: ©Michael Brown | Dreamstime.com
Clipart of Teepees and Totem Pole are in the public domain.

Disclaimer: This is a work of fiction. The characters, incidents and dialogue are products of the author's imagination and are not to be construed as real. Any resemblance to actual events or persons living or dead is entirely coincidental.

Extreme care has been taken by the author to ensure that all information presented in this book is accurate and up to date at the time of publishing. Neither the author nor the publisher can be held responsible for any errors or omissions. Additionally, neither is any liability assumed for damages resulting from the use of the information contained herein.

Publisher: CCB Publishing
              British Columbia, Canada
              www.ccbpublishing.com

To my son Stephen, who died from Leukemia at fourteen, and who loved to fish at The Lake of the Woods.

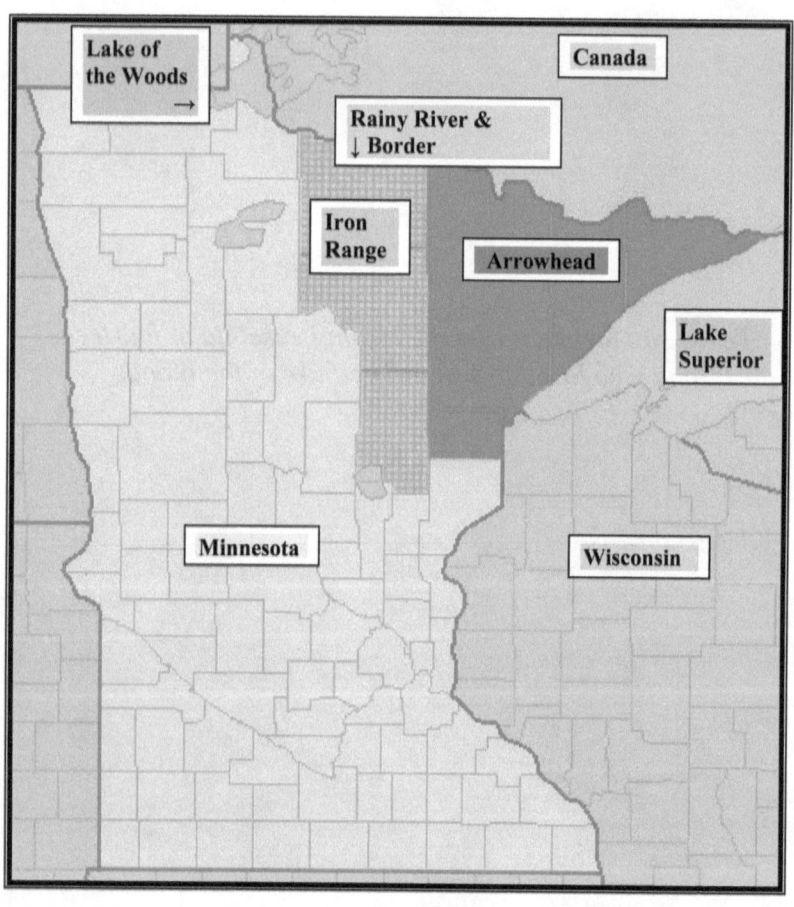

The Arrowhead Country

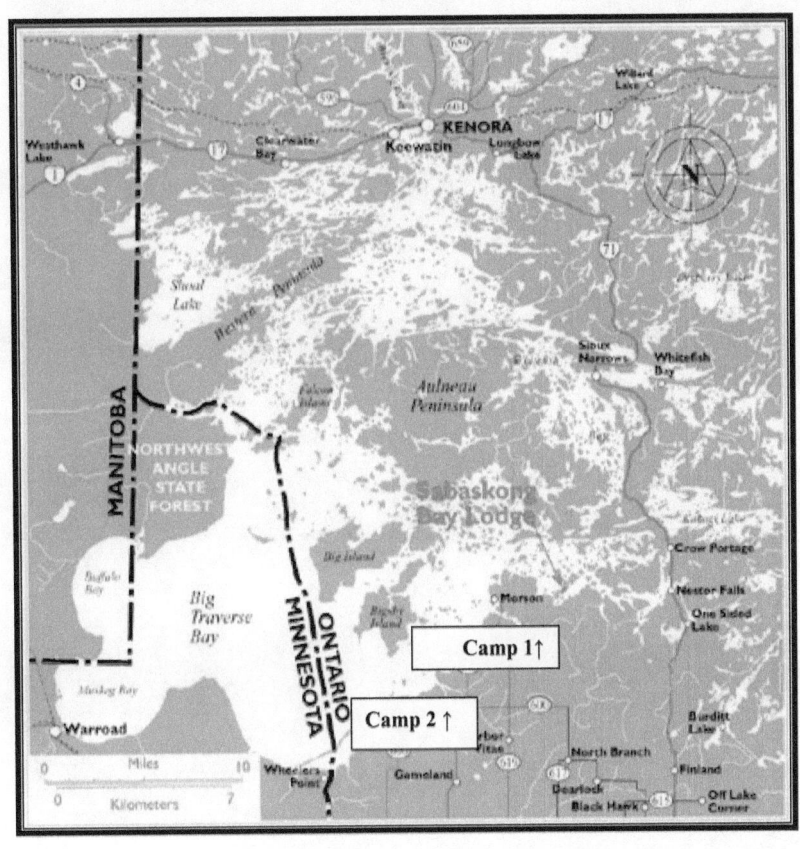

Lake of the Woods

Chapter 1

The north shore of Lake Superior, from Duluth to Thunder Bay forms the beginning of a very large wilderness area that's commonly referred to as the Boundary Waters, from which hundreds of tributaries empty into Lake Superior, some from as far away as James Bay in Ontario to Lake Winnipeg in Manitoba. One of the larger tributaries is the Rainy River, which flows from the southeastern tip of Lake of the Woods, which is located in north-central Minnesota, and Canada. This Rainy River also serves as a natural border between Canada and the United States, cutting its way southeast for more than two hundred miles before it finally reaches Lake Superior, some fifty miles southwest of Thunder Bay. From the southeastern tip of the Lake of the Woods this intercontinental border cuts across this lake to its mid-western shoreline, splitting the lake between these two countries. Between the Rainy River and Lake Superior's northern shoreline is a beautiful wilderness area that is shaped like the head of an arrow called the Arrowhead Country.

Although several mining companies had previously found vast deposits of high grade iron ore throughout much of northern Minnesota, this large Minnesota Iron Range soon became seriously depleted and depressed because of the world's huge demand for high quality iron ore. And although vast reserves of taconite, a flint-like rock containing thirty to fifty percent low-grade iron ore had been discovered in the Arrowhead Country back in 1870, it was initially considered worthless because extracting pure iron from the granite was found to be far too difficult and costly. Then in the 1940s, the process of extracting and upgrading taconite by "pelletizing" the iron into briquette-like pellets was discovered, causing the Reserve Mining Company to build a taconite processing plant at Silver Bay, on Lake Superior. As a result, by the late 1950s, they were producing and shipping up to 10 million tons of pellets a year, while irresponsibly disposing of the remaining powdered rock called tailings into Lake Superior.

The Ojibwe Annishinaabe or the Chippewa Indians, which is a white man's term, own reservations in both the United State's Arrowhead Country and the Canadian Boundary waters. Ojibwe means to heat or to pucker-up, which was derived from a description of the puckered seams on the Ojibwe moccasins. In the United States, the Ojibwe Indians call these boundary waters the Noopiming Boundary Waters while Canadians refer to this lake filled area as the Quetico Boundary Waters. For many years the Indian tribes had previously mined and processed this low grade iron ore to make their knives and hatchets, but with this new processing plant they soon found employment processing taconite at Silver Bay. They'd also made hatchets from copper, which was very plentiful in this area. Copper was obtained from a mineral called Malaxite, which the Indian's heated to 1,100 degrees Fahrenheit by forcing air into the flame and then pouring the melted copper into hatchet or knife molds. In doing this, they were totally unaware of the inevitable arsenic poisoning that occurred, and in doing this, many tribe members became ill from this arsenic poison. In processing iron ore, they also became ill from the dangerous taconite dust like particles that inevitably found their way into their lungs, often causing cancer.

Although the Indians in this area were mostly Ojibwe, there were several other tribes such as the Algonquin, the Ottawa, and the Cree Indians who were all friendly and spoke the same Alogonquian language. The Blackfeet Indians of Montana and Manitoba also spoke Alogonquian, but they were located farther to the west. The Dakota Tribes, commonly referred to as the nomadic Sioux, were scattered throughout this entire general area as well as the Upper Mississippi Valley, North and South Dakota and Ontario. They only spoke the Siouan language, and to make things worse, these Sioux were fierce warriors and a constant threat to the Ojibwe Annishinaabe. Sometimes these nomadic Sioux war parties could be found as far north as the Sioux Narrows on Lake of the Woods and they always presented a problem to the other tribes. Historically, there had been many skirmishes between the Sioux and these many other tribes that were often lumped together as the Ojibwe Annishinaabe. And although iron and copper were important natural resources to all these tribes, gold was seldom if ever found in this area, and therefore had never become an issue to fight over; however, this novel does focus on an unusual source of gold and how its location was secretly protected by three young men, one of which had accidentally claimed the first shiny gold nugget near the eastern shore of The Lake of the Woods.

* * * * *

This is a big mistake, Bill Warner thought as he motored out from Nestor Falls into the open water of Lake of the Woods. *At this speed, It will take us all day to get to Split Rock,* he was thinking to himself as he repeatedly tried to get the boat to rise above the water line, and move at a normal speed. Finally he shouted over the straining motor, "This isn't going to work!" With the water pushing against the bow of his seventeen foot tri hull it looked more like a barge than a sleek inboard, and after several more fruitless attempts, Bill cursed in frustration. "We're way too heavy!"

Although the hull of his boat was some thirty inches deep, the heavier waves were hitting within only a few inches of the top edge of the boat, and as he glared back at the large rolled up tent, several boxes of food, three or four tanks of water and gas, a metal cook stove, and a variety of gold mining equipment he whispered so the others could hear. *If we get into some rough water, we'll really have our hands full with all this gear weighing us down. And three two hundred pound passengers aren't exactly helping us any.*

Finally he just sat back letting the motor idle, while trying to figure out what to do next. Biting at the corner of his mouth he scowled at Dave and Ed before taking off his hat and scratching his head. "I should have known better," he snarled just as the wind valiantly slapped a huge wave over the side of the boat, forcing him to drop his hat on the floor and grab hold of the windshield with both hands.

Yes, Bill Warner had agreed with his two close friends to take the summer off from college so they could hunt gold, and his jaw tightened and his blue eyes became even more intense as another gust of wind swirled his blond sun-bleached hair in every direction. Turning to face both Dave and Ed, his right hand automatically grabbed for the back of his chair for support while the other rubbed the short stubble of a beard on his tan face. Still kind of biting on the inside of his cheek he stood silent, trying to decide if they should turn back or not.

Dave Olson's round face seemed frozen in a grin as he chuckled out loud. "What the hell — maybe we ought to pull Nelson behind the boat," he laughed, trying to ease the tension.

With that, Ed Nelson shook his head. "Oh sure - you're twice as big as I am, and you'd float a hell of a lot better, you smart ass."

Dave was as wide as he was tall, but all muscle, and he responded with a huge laugh. "All right, let's not get into a fight before we even get started.

During the last few summers Dave had worked for a U.S. Canadian mining firm that required he survive alone in the north woods in search of copper. His face was usually very tan but permanently scared from his childhood pox marks, and with his crew cut it gave him the undeserved appearance of a Chicago bouncer in an all night bar on Clark Street.

Ed Nelson was taller than Dave and almost frail by comparison, and to make things worse he wore heavy horned rimmed glasses and his long straight brown hair was swirling in every direction, making him look like a wimp while he struggled to put his baseball hat on backwards so the next gust of wind wouldn't whisk it into the lake again.

"Look, we've only got a couple of options." Bill growled. "We can go back and unload half of this stuff, and make two trips, or we can rent a second boat to help us get there in a reasonable length of time. And since we can't afford to rent a second boat for the entire summer, we should probably make a couple of trips, don't you think?"

"Wait a minute," Dave shouted over the wind, raising one arm high in the air to get their attention.

Dave was always quick with a solution to almost any dilemma, because of his north woods experience, where he'd often made quick decisions without any warning.

"Aren't we trying to sneak out there without being noticed, so we won't have any trouble with the Indians?"

"Alright," Bill agreed. "So what do you suggest we do?"

"I suggest we get out our fishing poles and troll our way out there, just as fast as this old barge will go. Haven't we got all the time in the world? That way we'll look more like fisherman than prospectors, and we won't be threatening those Indians who believe this is their sacred turf. Isn't that why we're sneaking out here by boat this time, so they won't chase us off what they think is their domain? When I went in there before, I hiked in from *Caliper Lake*, and I made those Indians so nervous they followed me every step of the way without my ever knowing it. In fact, I thought they were going to kill me when they woke me up that morning, and I couldn't get out of there fast enough, even with all my written authorizations they completely ignored."

"God all Friday, it'll take us ten hours to get out there at this speed," Bill snarled, still trying to figure out another solution.

"So what's wrong with that?" Dave once again chuckled. "We're in no big hurry. Don't you think it would be better if we quietly motor in at dusk anyway? That way we do it all in one trip, and we probably won't even be noticed."

"All right, if that's what you want - we'll do it your way," Bill said, flopping back down in his seat, obviously disturbed as he reached out and moved the throttle to a more relaxed trolling speed.

With that Ed reached for his fishing pole, and settled back for what was now going to be a much slower trip.

"Okay, I'm going to catch us some dinner on the way, in fact I can already taste those fresh Walleye" he smiled, throwing out his line behind the boat.

With that Bill laughed, turning his attention back to the direction he'd been heading as he once again sat tall behind the wheel, finally resigning himself to a much slower trip to *Split Rock* near *Bay Lodge*. And even though he wasn't sure this was the smartest solution, they at least were moving even though they were pushing a huge wall of water ahead of them. As they slowly moved from one island to another, Bill's thoughts drifted back to when Dave first shared his remarkable experience with them.

Dave had spent much of his time prospecting for copper mines during his vacation from college over the last few years, and during his assignment last year, he'd been asked to search out a very remote and new area just east of Lake of the Woods. While he was collecting his usual mineral samples, he focused his search primarily on locations around Log Creek and Caliper Lake. Then towards the end of the summer, he moved further west along the Grassy River, which was next to a small Canadian Indian Reservation, eventually finding his way to what he'd identified as the Split Rock River. In that he'd initially entered the forest near Caliper Lake, he'd probably hiked some ten miles or more before reaching this remote location, which was about five to ten miles south of Lake of the Woods. Previously, Dave had always worked in the Arrowhead Boundary Waters of Minnesota, where he was familiar with the wilderness and the local Indians who all knew him very well, but for some reason he felt very uneasy in this strange new Canadian forest. He wasn't as worried about the animals as he was about an unruly tribe of Indians he'd heard about when he stayed overnight in Nestor Falls. Then one day when he was gathering his copper samples, he was startled to find what appeared to be lava like silt along the Split Rock riverbank.

Could it be possible that there was once some kind of volcanic action here, he thought. Then later that same day, while he was bathing in this cold refreshing stream he noticed several shiny rocks reflecting the sun's rays. After he gathered up several of them he stuck them under the canvas floor of his tent for safe keeping. And although he felt it was highly unlikely they were gold, *they sure looked like gold,* he'd thought. In any event, he'd decided that he'd have them checked out when he got back home, even though he'd never heard of gold ever being found in this part of the country. Then the following morning, Dave awoke to a terrible noise outside the tent and after he hurriedly crawled out of his sleeping bag, he found four defiant Indians methodically trashing his campsite. When they were finished, he was told in no uncertain terms to leave immediately, or risk not leaving at all. After he awkwardly tried to explain that he was doing government work, and showing them his papers, he realized that made no difference at all and they only became more irritated with him. Needless to say, he took their advice, but later he found out that those shiny rocks were not only gold nuggets, but the purity of the gold was extremely high. In fact, these few nuggets netted him close to one thousand dollars, which paid for his college tuition and much more that year. After telling Bill and Ed of his unusual find, they'd all agreed to take the next summer off, and go look for gold in the Split Rock River. But this time, Dave recommended they hike into the area from the mouth of that river on Lake of the Woods, acting as fishermen rather than surveying the land for copper. This way, they'd hopefully not attract all the attention he'd previously received with that unruly tribe while he was searching for copper the previous year.

Yes, it was important they sneak in quietly, Bill was thinking to himself as Ed suddenly screamed,

"Get the net! I've got our dinner on the end of this line."

After Ed landed a beautiful five pound Walleye, all three laughed and once again seemed excited by what lay ahead. After Dave placed their dinner in the live tank, they all sat back to once again enjoy the tranquility of the huge pine trees and solid granite cliffs that made up the many islands in this huge lake. "This section of the lake is nothing like the open water to the west," Bill explained. *In fact this is one of the most beautiful Lakes in Canada,* he thought to himself, as he turned his attention to his map to confirm their location, trying to determine how much further they had to go. Then later that afternoon, they finally reached Split Rock Bay, and it was now only a short distance before they'd reach their campsite next to the waterfall at the mouth of the river. Since Bill had previously fished the falls by the mouth of the river, he remembered there was a huge reed bed that covered the shoreline. *This would provide ideal cover for them,* he thought, *but they'd also have to push there way through all those mosquito infested reeds to find a good spot where they could hide the boat.*

"All right, you better get covered with mosquito repellent," Bill explained, as they approached the waterfall and that dense reed bed that covered the entire backwater area.

At first Bill tried to motor through the reeds that were blocking their path, but that was impossible, so Dave and Ed both climbed up on the bow and physically pushed and pulled their way forward. After what seemed like an eternity, they eventually found a good landing spot fairly close to where they'd planned to camp near the rushing waterfall, and although the mosquitoes repellent had helped some, they all had more than enough bites from the huge swarms of mosquitoes. As they pulled the boat onto the sandy beach, they hurriedly unloaded their equipment by passing things up to the higher ground, where there were far fewer mosquitoes to fight. Then after a quick search of the area, Ed shouted, "this looks like a good campsite over here by the stream," swinging his ax as if clearing a space for their tent. Since they'd all brought guns for their protection this time, they paused just long enough to strap them on before setting up camp. While Ed gathered firewood, Dave and Bill struggled to raise the large canvas tent, which had taken up so much room in the boat. Then after they were finished, Bill worked his way back through the swarms of mosquitoes to secure the boat by zipping on the boat's canvas top and raising the motor just as the last splinter of sunlight faded behind the tall dense pines. Bill's huge tent was a real luxury, some twelve by sixteen feet in size with screened openings and waterproof flooring, and the green color blended well with the trees so that it was hardly noticeable in spite of its size. But getting settled in the dark was no picnic, and by the time they set up their table, and raised their ice chests on pulleys so they wouldn't be trashed by bear, it was pitch dark. Finally after they all settled down around a warm campfire, the steady noise of the stream quickly put them at peace with Mother Nature, and since Ed had caught the fish, Dave was unanimously elected to cook dinner. While Bill and Ed watched Dave work by the fire they all sipped on a cold beer, visiting about the days ahead.

"Boy, there's nothing better than fresh Walleye cooked over a campfire," Dave grinned, scrapping the last bit of food from his plate. "I'm going to sleep like a baby," he mumbled after dowsing the flames and zipping up the tent screen, where they all collapsed on their sleeping bags.

The next morning, as Bill awoke, he looked around the tent and could see that Ed was already up, so he dressed and went out to see what their campsite looked like in the daylight. Ed had started a campfire, but he was nowhere to be found. In fact, the morning fog was so dense, Bill could barely see the stream, and since the grass was covered with due it wasn't difficult to follow Ed's tracks to where he found him crouching behind a tree, staring at the swirling backwater.

"Hush," Ed whispered, raising his hand to point at the backwater area that was completely covered by this thick eerie haze of morning fog. "I'm watching some beavers," he whispered.

Quietly Bill crouched down beside him, and it took only a moment before a beaver glided smoothly through the water, only stopping to slap its tail before diving beneath the surface. As the beaver reappeared on the shore, he quickly waddled into the woods to find a branch, which he then carefully added to their already large beaver dam. As Bill and Ed watched, fascinated by his work, the sun began to slowly eat through the heavy fog and then suddenly a large section of blue sky appeared. *Ed must have been up since the crack of dawn*, Bill thought, as he noticed an outdoor biffy he'd quietly built with some logs while he and Dave were sleeping.

When they finally returned to camp, they found Dave was already busy cooking breakfast. "I think we found a pretty good camp site, don't you?" Dave garbled in a voice that was still half asleep.

"It looks great," Bill smiled.

Dave had been boiling coffee in a coffee can, and he hurriedly grabbed it off the fire with a pot holder as the grounds boiled over and sizzled in the flames. Setting his makeshift coffee pot on a rock, he let the remaining coffee grounds settle before pouring their coffee.

"The bacon and eggs are almost done," he yelled. "You better get a plate and eat while things are good and hot."

After breakfast, Dave spread out his map, and pointed out the location where he'd found gold the previous summer.

"It should be right about here," he said, authoritatively tapping his finger on the map. "Do you think you're up to looking for some gold today?" He grinned.

As he looked for a response, they both smiled and nodded enthusiastically. "I'd guess it's about a six mile hike from here," Dave continued. "Why don't we pack a lunch and some tools and head out," he said, wiping the remaining grease from the frying pan with a paper towel, which flared up when he threw it on the hot coals.

"I'm ready," Bill said, "but we better be sure we put out that fire before we leave."

"My God, it's almost nine o'clock," Dave yelled, looking at his watch.

Chapter 2

The three of them found the hike along the river a torturous ordeal as they cut and chopped their way through the dense underbrush that no human had ever before disturbed. Several times they crossed the stream, to see if there was any kind of trail they could follow, but as they hiked deeper into the woods the underbrush only became thicker. At times, they even had to use an ax to cut through thick brush as black flies swarmed out of every clump, biting their bare arms and necks relentlessly.

"Holly shit," Dave shouted. "I walked this damned stream from the other direction last year, and I never saw anything like this!" Finally he stretched his arms up toward the sky and drew in a deep breath as he shook his head in disgust,

"I just can't believe this!"

Both Bill and Ed looked at Dave, doubting him for the first time. "Let's just sit down and talk a minute," Bill said, equally frustrated by what they were finding.

"Dave, do you think you made a mistake?" Ed asked, wiping the sweat from his forehead with his forearm and swirling his red-checkered handkerchief at a huge black fly that was determined to take another piece of flesh from his already swollen neck.

"This is not the same stream I walked last year," Dave snarled, totally upset.

"Well, what are we going to do?" Bill scowled.

"I don't know." Dave whispered, tightening his jaw and shaking his head hopelessly. "And besides that, this stream seems to be drying up the further we go, which is really beginning to bother me." As he rubbed his hand over his unshaved chin, he once again reached into his vest for his map. Carefully he unfolded it, spreading it out on the ground as his finger slowly traced and retraced the line that was supposed to be the Split Rock River. Finally he looked up as his eyes narrowed and his lips tightened. "According to this, there's not another stream within ten miles," he growled, pointing as he held out the map so they could see what he was talking about. "We must have hiked at least five miles by now, so we should be getting close to where I found the gold, yet it looks like this stream's about to disappear." Standing up, he groaned. "Things just aren't right," he muttered, starring at the dense underbrush that lay ahead. Then reaching out to help his equally exhausted companions to their feet, he took another deep breath. "Let's go a little further, before we give up," he mumbled.

After following the small stream for another excruciating mile of dense underbrush, they finally came to an open area that looked more like a marsh than a stream.

"I just can't believe this," Dave mumbled defiantly, biting at his upper lip in disgust and confusion. "I'm absolutely sure that this is not the stream I walked last year! There was more water in that stream than we've seen all morning."

Pausing to check the directions on his compass, he stood utterly bewildered, obviously trying to figure out what to do next.

"I never thought you'd get lost in these woods," Bill laughed. "Perhaps your mind is playing tricks on you. Haven't you seen anything that even looks slightly familiar?"

"Hell no," Dave grimaced, utterly puzzled by this strange turn of events. "I know what I saw, and there's got to be another answer to this," he whispered. "I'd have to be an idiot to be fooled into believing this is the same stream I saw last year."

With that, Ed stared at his watch. "Well, it's taken us almost four hours to get this far, and if we start back now, it'll probably be dusk by the time we get back to camp."

"Yes, I guess we should start back," Dave finally admitted. "We're not prepared to stay out here all night," he said as he turned and began to walk toward camp. "But I'm going to have to somehow figure this thing out," he grimaced. "Tomorrow, we should maybe branch out from here and try to find that lost stream that I know exists, cause this sure as hell isn't it," he painfully admitted, pinching his lips tightly together as he turned and headed toward camp in defeat. "Damn it, this may well be the Split Rock River, but it certainly isn't the stream I found gold in last year."

With that Ed looked at Bill, rolling his eyes. "I've been duped many times in my life, but this would be the biggest dupe ever if you've been pulling our leg all along," Ed unsympathetically snarled, undoubtedly questioning Dave for the first time.

"Hey, you gotta believe me!" Dave growled back rebelliously, realizing the seriousness of the situation they were in. "Just bear with me. I'm gonna figure this thing out."

With that, both Bill and Ed turned without saying a word and continued walking back toward camp, as Dave followed, muttering and cussing under his breath almost every step of the way.

The trail home was much easier as they traced their way back over the beaten path they'd forged earlier. This time it took only two hours, and they all decided to skip dinner as they fell exhausted into their sleeping bags, still sweaty and fully dressed.

The next morning they seriously discussed things again, while ravenously eating their breakfast and stretching out some of their aching muscles, finally agreeing to spend the day recovering from yesterday's grueling ordeal. Ed even suggested it might be best if they forget the whole thing and return home, but Dave persisted, convincing them to stay and at least try to search for his magic river that he was sure was there somewhere and was filled with gold nuggets. He even suggested they might go back to Caliper Lake, and take the very same trail he'd taken last year, but that was only as a last resort and would almost certainly attract the Indians again.

"Maybe we should go back to where we were yesterday and each take a compass and walk five miles in different directions," Bill suggested. "That's if you think we were anywhere near the trail you walked last year."

"I swear there's another stream out there, and I know we had to be pretty darn close to it," Dave frowned boldly, while placing a large log on the fire. "And you know what? It wouldn't be the first time that I found a map to be wrong," sensing that both Bill and Ed had become much more skeptical of what he'd been telling them all along.

"All right, I'll go along with you one more time," Ed shouted. "But if we don't find something tomorrow I'm heading home, with or without you guys." he said, demanding Dave's agreement.

After several moments of silence, Dave looked up and stared back. "All right, but I'm going to prove to you I know what I'm talking about," he replied, slowly forcing his aching body up and walking to his sleeping bag where he could lay down and think things over.

The following morning they packed food and water and their rolled up sleeping bags, intending to stay no more than one night away from their base camp. Dave had laid awake much of the night studying his maps over and over, tracing and retracing his markings on the very same map he'd used the previous year.

"Worst case is, we had to be within three to five miles of where I hiked last year, and we're bound to find something if we all branch out from that spot we were at," Dave explained, slowly lifting his backpack to his shoulders. "My gut feeling is that river has to be to the west. We could head southwest from here, but we'd be blazing a new trail, so my suggestion is we retrace our old trail and each separately head out from where we were the other day, just like Bill suggested."

This time Dave took the lead, reaching the spring fed marsh in less than two hours, while stopping to rest only once.

"It looks like the underbrush thins out toward the west, so hopefully you won't need to chop your way any longer, but I recommend you each mark your trail frequently," Dave explained, as he tied a red marker to a tall branch that was clearly visible from the west end of this rather large clearing. "Remember it's an overcast day, so you'll really have to rely on your compass."

Dave planned to head in a southwest direction and Bill to the northwest, while Ed would walk between them, directly toward the west, and they all agreed to return to Dave's marker in two hours. If any one of them did not return by then, the others were to wait one hour before giving any type of gun signal, since Dave felt it important they keep their presence in the area a secret.

"And for God sake, if you feel you're lost, don't keep walking," Dave explained. "Just stop and wait for us to come and find you."

Bill had been walking at a good pace for almost an hour before he heard what sounded like rushing water off in the distance. Although he knew better, he began to run in the direction of the noise, something you should never do in the wilderness. And then suddenly, right in front of him stood a huge black bear that seemed just as startled as he was. Standing motionless, Bill tried to look as tall as he could while slowly reaching for his magnum. Once his hand contacted the handle, it was out of his holster in less time than it would take to blink your eye, and as he slowly raised both arms with no eye contact, the bear stood up on his hind legs and snarled with his hair raised on his back, poised to attack at the slightest provocation.

"Get out of here," Bill shouted loudly, while realizing that if the bear did decide to attack he'd have time for only one shot. To Bill, the bear's challenge seemed to last for an eternity, while he intentionally tried to avoid eye contact, which would surely cause this monster to attack, a characteristic of most wild animals when challenged in a sudden confrontation like this. While Bill held his arms up high to look as big as possible, he realized he needed to carefully lower one arm and level his gun at the bear's head, just in case. And as he did that, the bear's stare down finally came to an end as the animal slowly lowered his towering frame to the ground. Turning and walking away, the bear only stopping to look back as if to once more evaluate this unusual animal that'd suddenly interrupted his search for food and wild berries. Only after the bear disappeared into the forest, did Bill gradually wipe his forehead and take a deep breath, muttering to himself softly, *that was way to close.*

Bill's first thought was to turn around and head back, but he felt certain that Dave's stream was just over the next rise, so he proceeded, but far more cautiously this time.

Finally he found himself staring at Dave's stream right before his eyes. "There it is," he chocked, suppressing a yell for joy as he tightly clenching both fists. "I'll be darned, Dave was right," he whispered.

The stream looked just like Dave had described it, filled with swirling rapids and backwater currents. And as he crouched by the edge of the bank the sun suddenly broke through the clouds for only a moment, as if to celebrate his good fortune.

Meanwhile, Ed had also been hearing a peculiar noise that he couldn't quite identify, but he trudged on rather discouraged by not having found anything during the first hour. But continuing further, he noticed the noise was becoming louder with each step.

What is that noise? Could it be the wind or maybe a train off in the distance? He thought to himself. Then as he roughly pushed aside a clump of brush, he spotted a huge granite cliff several hundred yards away. Increasing his pace, he suddenly felt both fear and excitement at what might lie ahead.

I hope that noise isn't some Indian tribe, he thought to himself. This had been in the back of his mind much of the morning, and he'd been thinking of what he might do if any Indians confronted him, mainly now while he was all alone.

Then suddenly he found himself standing and looking up at a solid granite cliff that towered over him.

"That's gotta be a waterfall I'm hearing." he whispered, his excitement growing with every minute. Hurriedly he worked his way along the base of the cliff to a steep crevice he thought he might be able to climb without falling, but as he looked at his watch he realized he'd already seriously exceeded the halfway point in time, and he paused to evaluate the situation before starting any dangerous climb.

I better return for help, he thought. *In fact I could fall getting up there and that would be a disaster.* Pausing only to once again confirm the sound of running water, he quickly turned and started back. This time his pace was filled with renewed energy, while stopping frequently to check for the marks he'd carved in the trees.

Boy, am glad I brought my compass, he thought, as he kept missing marker after marker. At times he felt completely lost, but then after what seemed like an eternity he'd finally find another mark.

It was now well past their deadline they'd set, and Dave and Bill were getting very concerned by Ed's absence. Dave was just about to start tracking Ed's markers, when he saw him suddenly appear from a patch of birch trees far to the south of where he'd originally started out.

"Thank God," Dave whispered to Bill. "Hey Ed, we were getting worried about you," he shouted.

As Ed approached them, they could see the relief on his face, along with a smile that suggested he'd also found something.

"Just wait until you hear what I have to tell you," he joyfully smiled, clearly relieved by finally finding his way back to where he'd started from earlier that day. For the next half hour they ate lunch and talked about the cliff, the hidden waterfall, and laughed over Bill's frightening confrontation with that huge black bear.

"I told you guys we'd figure this thing out!" Dave slyly chuckled, grinning from ear to ear. "Now I'm more determined than ever. And Damn it, we're now gonna find some gold nuggets," he laughed, once again marking his map where he'd suspected the mysterious lost river was located. "It all makes sense," he said. "I bet those map makers just assumed it was the Split Rock River." Then he paused to think a moment.

"Let's try to make it to Ed's wall, and we can camp there tonight."

As they gathered their packs, they continued to jabber, and during the silent moments it was obvious they were hopefully thinking about the gold they were surely going to find, once they found this hidden stream. During their brisk hike, they also joked about chopping their way along that dried up river as their obvious enthusiasm was rekindled with every step they took.

"It looks like we might have to move our campsite and the boat." Dave explained.

"Yes," Bill agreed, "but first we'll need to determine where this new river empties into the lake."

Suddenly Ed pointed straight ahead. "There it is," he grinned, stopping just long enough to stare at the jagged cliff he'd been describing over and over.

"It doesn't look so big from here," Dave laughed. Then with a little more concern, he whispered, "But I don't recall seeing anything like that last year!"

Once again, it took only a short time before they were standing at the foot of the cliff.

"That surely sounds like a waterfall to me," Dave whispered, "there's no mistake about that. Now all we have to do is figure out how to get up there so we can see it."

After much searching, they finally found a crevice that looked climbable, and they quickly started the difficult task of slowly working their way to the top. After more than a few scrapes and bruises, the three tired climbers cautiously peeked over the edge of the cliff, where they stared in awe at a large bowl of cascading rapids that seemed to be bubbling right out of the earth itself.

"Oh my God," Dave shouted. "I've never seen anything like this in my entire life."

As Ed and Bill pulled them self up to where they could see better, they both mumbled, "Oh my God - I can't believe this."

"That has to be an aquifer," Bill shouted. "That water's coming right up out of the ground. I remember seeing one of these in Austin, Texas — it was called The Edward's Aquifer," he explained over the noise of the rushing water. "And look at that mist it's making over the pond — it looks like it's bubbling right out of the bowls of the earth."

"I've heard that rivers can travel hundreds of miles underground, but this is unreal," Dave explained, pausing to take a deep breath. "So that's where the lava silt and gold must be coming from. In fact, I wouldn't be surprised if this waters coming from as far away as the Canadian Rockies. That's the only way lava silt could be found in this part of the country."

Finally all three of them just sat completely silent, absorbing every detail of the remarkable phenomenon that was unfolding right in front of them under an equally spectacular sunset, and it soon became obvious that words were unable to describe any of their feelings.

After several minutes had passed, the spell of the moment was shattered by the repeated clicking of Ed's camera, as they finally decided to climb down into this huge bowl, where the water was wildly dumping into Dave's magic stream.

"All these cliffs must have been pushed up through the crust of the earth years ago," Bill whispered, still out of breath, as all three of them awkwardly slid their way down to the edge of the churning water that was slowly swirling in a large circle. As they stood entranced by the power surrounding them, the cooling mist washed the sweat from their faces, and in a strange but magical way it seemed to offer strength to their tired bodies. The entire pool was at least twenty yards across, and as they cautiously walked along the edge of the pond, they felt as if they were in some strange hypnotic trance. The whole experience had left them with a euphoric feeling, but also an ominous respect and fear of the magical things that were noticeably overwhelming each of them.

Those Indians must have known about this? Dave thought, as they worked their way around to the cascading stream rushing out the mouth of this most unusual pond that sat in what looked like a bombed out crater. Finally they walked to a more peaceful location down stream, where they could camp for the night, just as the sun was falling below the horizon and they all hurriedly collected wood for a fire that would provide their security for the night.

Chapter 3

Bear Claw was the Chief of the Ojibwe Annishinaabe Indians living on the Red Lake Reservation, which was located on the United State's side of the boarder along the western shoreline of The Lake of the Woods. Both Canada and the United States had granted the Indians the sole right to net fish from this lake's abundant supply of Walleye, and the Ojibwe tribe made much of their living by selling the fish they netted from the large open waters at the south end of this huge lake. Bear Claw, and his small tribe of Ojibwe Indians also maintained a fish processing plant at Wheeler's Point, where the lake emptied into the Rainy River, which was only six miles north of Baudette, Minnesota. When the tribe was netting near the eastern shore, they always stayed at their smaller Canadian Reservation at the mouth of the Grassy River. On this Reservation, there was a single dirt road that took them south to Wheelers Point, which was about eight miles southwest from where Dave, Bill and Ed were camping at Split Rock Falls.

"Please tell us the story about *Kitchimanidoo*, the children shouted as they pulled on Bear Claw's deerskin pants leg."

With that Bear Claw smiled, as he casually sat down on a huge log bench near the fire.

"All right, but you must promise me you'll go right home and go to sleep when I'm finished."

"Yes, we promise," they shouted in unison as they all snuggled close together, tucking their legs under them and leaning forward in anticipation of what was about to take place.

Bear Claw was in his late seventies, and his face was tanned and wrinkled from the strong winds that were almost always blowing over Lake of the Woods. In fact his wrinkled skin looked much like the leather band he always wore around his forehead, holding back his long gray hair that was tied together behind his head. Bear Claw always enjoyed returning to their Red Lake Reservation after a hard week's work, and the children always looked forward to hearing the Chief's remarkable stories about their tribe's history, which was of course a very special treat for them. Although his joints ached, he awkwardly moved each leg into a comfortable position where they could absorb the heat from the warm and inviting fire. As he lit his pipe, he looked up and blew a huge puff of smoke into the air, as if he was calling upon the Great Spirit *Kitchimanidoo* for assistance.

"Many moons have passed since *Kitchimanidoo,* the Great Spirit, approached my father Chief Black Thunder as he and his hunting party slept on the eastern shore of the great Lake of the Woods. "

Bear Claw usually spoke loudly as the Chief, but suddenly he lowered his voice to a whisper saying, "He came as a *Ma'iingan,*" raising both eyebrows and staring intently at each child sitting around the fire. "As you all know, a *Ma'iingan* is a great gray wolf."

With this the children's eyes widened as they cuddled even closer to one another.

"The *Ma'iingan* told Chief Black Thunder, that a great battle was about to be waged right on the very spot they were sleeping, and that many *Sioux Warriors* would attack their camp at the break of dawn."

"With that, the great Chief Black Thunder woke in a cold sweat as the great gray wolf suddenly disappeared from his dream, but he was sure that the *Ma'iingan* came to warn him of this great danger. Chief Black Thunder slowly looked around the camp, while the moon cast long frightening shadows from the trees that were blowing in the night wind. The fire's glowing coals were almost out, as Chief Thunder silently prayed to the *Great Spirit Kitchimanidoo. 'Oh Great Spirit, tell me what I should do.'* He pleaded."

With that Bear Claw took his pipe and loudly hit it against the log, causing some of the children to shudder as they huddled even closer together. While knocking the hot ashes to the ground, he sat silently staring at the children. Then finally, after he slowly reamed out his empty pipe, he continued.

"Black Thunder lay motionless for a while until the moon finally disappeared behind a cloud, and then he decided to slowly crawl on the ground to warn each member of his hunting party."

With this, Bear Claw hunched forward moving his arms as if he were crawling.

"By morning, the Ojibwe hunting party had prepared for the attack by filling their blankets with leaves and brush to look like they were sleeping — and while they crouched in the deep grass that lined the shore, they all waited for the attack. Black Thunder knew the *Great Spirit Kitchimanidoo* had sent the fog for their protection, which had suddenly replaced the wind, but this created an even more frightening and eerie feeling for his hunters as the morning light began to show."

As Bear Claw spoke, he crouched silently as if he himself was waiting for the attack.

"Suddenly Black Thunder and his tribe of hunters saw many shadows sneaking from the woods, with knives raised, ready to pounce on each sleeping figure."

As Bear Claw spoke, he drew his knife and raised it high above his head. Driving his knife into the log, the wide open eyes of the children starred in disbelief. Then after leaving his knife in the log, Bear Claw once again sat tall, before continuing.

"As the Sioux drove their knifes into the blankets, Black Thunder suddenly let out a blood curtailing war cry, and each member of his hunting party raised their bow and shot an arrow into the Sioux warrior that had stabbed their blanket."

With this, Bear Claw paused and raised both eyebrows.

"The Sioux were caught completely by surprise," he whispered, "and as the Sioux warriors fell to the ground, the Ojibwe reloaded and continued to shoot until they were almost certain that no Sioux warrior remained alive. Only three Ojibwe were slightly wounded when they approached the Sioux, and although unknown to the Ojibwe some Sioux had managed to escape. Then as they walked among the dead Sioux warriors, a strange light suddenly appeared in the sky."

With this, Bear Claw raised his arm and pointed to the east.

"Black Thunder and his hunting party stood staring at the light as it grew larger and larger, leaving a long tail of fire before it finally hit into the ground only a few miles away."

With this Bear Claw held out both hands and waved them in front of him.

"When this strange ball of fire hit the earth, the ground shook, and flames shot high into the air, as the Ojibwe hunters threw themselves to the ground face down in fear. Many of the brave hunters yelled this must be *Majaimanidoog,* which meant devil; while others yelled *Majimanidoo,* which meant a dark evil spirit."

Bear Claw slowly stood up and this time he reached out with both arms toward the sky.

"No — Black Thunder shouted, this is surely *Nanabozho*. Only a spirit full of tricks could cause such a celebration," Bear Claw shouted.

With this, the children cheered with joy, laughing loudly as they prodded one another, whispering *Nanabozho* to one another. Then Bear Claws slowly sat back on the log, before continuing.

"Black Thunder and his warriors felt it important to search out where the strange fire had landed, but it was a long, slow and tedious walk because their three wounded warriors slowed them down — yet they knew their trail was in the right direction as they followed the small plume of smoke that could still be seen in the sky where the strange light had hit the earth."

Bear Claw paused to refill his pipe, and after lighting it with a stick from the fire he once again blew smoke into the air, looking around just as if he was still searching for this strange fire that had dropped from the sky.

"Then suddenly the winds began to blow," he continued, "as dark clouds moved in to empty their rain they'd gathered over the great lake they'd just passed over, and soon there was no place to hide as lightning and thunder seemed to be everywhere. "

This time Bear Claw raised both arms above his head as if to protect himself from a storm.

"Surely this was a warning to stay away from the strange light in the sky. Then suddenly the rain stopped, and they could no longer see the smoke against the gray sky. With that, Black Thunder's hunters felt hopelessly lost and saddened for it now could be very difficult to find where the fire had landed. So they turned and began to head back to their camp when suddenly the hunters stopped, all staring at something that seemed to be blocking their path. 'Look,' one of the tribe members shouted, pointing in the direction they'd been walking. Off in the distance, the warriors could see *Ma'iingan,* the same great gray wolf that Black Thunder had seen in his dream."

With that Bear Claw once again lowered his voice as he stood up and gestured with his arm, "'Follow me,' the *Ma'iingan* seemed to be saying."

Each child's eyes were now frozen on Bear Claw, believing he really was the *Ma'iingan.*

"The hunting party was terrified, but cautiously followed the *Ma'iingan* until he suddenly disappeared at the foot of a huge rock filled pit that no one had ever seen before."

"This must be where the fire landed, the tribe members murmured to one another, as they found their way to where they could now see a large hole in the ground that had surely been created by this strange ball of fire they had all seen in the sky."

"Look, Black Thunder shouted. There in the center of the gouged out ground stood what looked like a huge ball of smoldering rock. Surely the Great Spirit has marked this land for us, so we will always know where our great battle was fought."

With this, Bear Claw again pounded his pipe loudly against the log, and before he put his pipe away, he whispered.

"And then it happened!"

Each child seemed suspended in mid air, as they waited for him to continue.

"What happened?" They all shouted.

"Steam began to rise around the large hot rock, curling high into the air, like a ghost swirling around them. Then suddenly there was a hissing like sound of a great serpent that grew louder and louder until the warrior's ears felt like they were going to split if they didn't cover them.

Then just as sudden as the noise stopped, they saw water spouting out of the ground, shooting everywhere, as if it had been trapped in the ground for many moons. It took only moments for the water to fill the hole in the earth as it began to flow as if it was anxious to reach our great fishing lake. Still in shock by what the warriors had all witnessed, they stood back safely so they were not washed away by the roaring stream as they watched this magic river bubble out of the earth and flow north toward the lake. The spray from the water seemed to be everywhere, feeling cold as ice on their face, as it cooled their sweat covered bodies while they watched this Great Spirit show off its power. As each of the tribe members tasted the water on their lips, it seemed to magically quench their thirst."

With that Bear Claw licked his lips, as if he himself had just quenched a deep thirst.

"Then one of the wounded warriors looked at his wounds and screamed in amazement. 'My wound is gone, I'm healed!'"

"As each of the wounded warriors looked at their wounds, they were shocked to see that all their injuries were completely healed."

"Chief Black Thunder stood up and shouted loudly above the noises of the rushing magic river."

"This is surely the work of the *Great Spirit Kitchimanido.* He has provided these sacred waters as our *Midewiwin,'* [medicine man]. We must keep this water secret from the Sioux, and the white man. We must never let them know of this spirit who saved our lives and healed our wounds."

Bear Claw then stood up and began to walk away, but after he took several steps he stopped and turned back to look at the children.

"Tonight, you can dream of this great gift the spirit has given us, but you must never speak about it with anyone other than an Annishinaabe Indian."

"Can we go see this Great Midewiwin Gift?" One child asked.

"Not until you are older. Its location must be kept secret, but soon our fisherman will be bringing a fresh supply of this magical water to our reservation, and you may all have a taste."

Chapter 4

After breakfast, Bill, Dave and Ed hurriedly packed for their hike to the mouth of this amazing stream that was fed by this remarkable aquifer. After walking less than a half mile, Dave stopped and pointed to a clearing.

"This is where the Indians threatened me and destroyed my camp site," Dave explained, his eyes studying the area. As Bill and Ed looked at Dave, it quickly became apparent his body recaptured some of the fear he'd experienced a year ago when they chased him out of here.

Nervously they all looked at each other, not knowing what they'd really do if they were again confronted by this same tribe of Indians.

"What are we going to do, if they do find us?" Ed asked.

"Well, we'll just tell them we're fishing, and if they don't like it, that's their problem," Dave scoffed. "But this time, I'm at least going to find out if these Indians are Chippewwa or Sioux. If they're Chippewwa, I'll tell them I'm a good friend of Chief White Cloud from the *Arrowhead Country*. And if that doesn't work, I've got my Ruger Super Blackhawk .44 Magnum persuader right here on my waist," he said, patting his gun case. "But let's hope that never happens, and I think it will be the best of all worlds if we can just keep a low profile. Remember, I spent ninety days in this forest before they kicked my butt out of here last year."

"Do you think they know there's gold in this stream?" Bill asked.

"I'm not sure they even suspected that, they just wanted me out of here for some damned reason."

"Well, if we're going to tell them we're fishing," Bill said thoughtfully rubbing at his rough chin, "I think it would be wise if we set up camp near the lake. That way they'll have a tough time questioning our presence, and we can sneak up stream whenever we want to look for gold."

"I agree. And if we camp near the lake, they'll have a tough time chasing us out," Dave said. "They don't dare start chasing U.S. fishermen off the lake, or the Game Wardens will be all over them."

Ed nodded. "Yes, but before we even start searching for any gold, we still have to move our boat and campsite to the mouth of this stream, so maybe we should get busy."

"Hey," Dave shouted. "You've got to let me at least find one nugget, before we do that," he grinned. "I still have to prove to you guys that I know what I'm talking about — don't I?"

With that, Dave walked leather boots and all into the stream while staring at the bottom as if he expected to see that same sparkle he saw when he was bathing in this cold water a year ago. Several times he reached down, grabbing at a suspicious rock, only to turn and quickly throw it away in disgust. He even tried panning with his hands, in the shallow water, but to no avail.

Damn, this might be harder than I thought, he mumbled. *But I know gold's here somewhere,* he whispered to himself.

"I think Ed's right." Bill finally interrupted Dave. "Let's find the mouth of this stream and move our camp site first, and then we can search for gold as long as we'd like. I never expected it to be like picking cherries off a tree anyway. Come on Dave, you look silly as hell the way you're going at it now, we need to get our equipment and do this thing right."

"Yah, I guess you're right," Dave laughed, slipping in the mud several times as he climbed out of the water. "Let's go find the mouth of this river and then get back to camp before its dark," he snickered as he squeezed water from his wet pants legs.

As they walked along this stream it was a much easier hike than the previous Split Rock fiasco, and it only took about an hour before they were looking out over an expansive view of the lake, which Bill quickly identified as the *Sabaskong Bay*.

"This huge *Sabaskong Bay* is just to the north of the very large open body of water to our south," Bill explained. "And to the west of the *Sabaskong* there are hundreds of islands that one can easily get lost in. Even though the *Sabaskong* looks peaceful today, I've always been very cautious of this section of the lake, because those sudden winds can whip around the islands and kick up some dangerous waves in an instant — and those waves can sometimes reach five to ten feet high in this peaceful water we're looking at right now. Several times I've been forced to find refuge on one of those islands to the west, so it's very easy for me to remember this crazy part of the lake."

As Bill studied Dave's map, it took him only moments to determine that they were at the eastern end of a very small bay between the great open water of Lake of the Woods and the *Sabaskong,* a place called *Hay's Bay*, where Bill had once fished with an Indian guide. They were also surprised that a dense growth of tall reeds completely hid the entire mouth of their magic river. Actually, the stream had become much wider at the mouth, and had they tried to find it from the lake, they would never have even suspected their magic river was here.

"Know wonder nobody has found this remarkable stream from the lake," Bill smirked, glancing over Dave's shoulder at his map. "If you look at where we're standing, they've only marked a small line on the map, which would have never even suggested there was a river here."

"You're absolutely right," Dave whistled. "Those damned map makers sure missed this one. I just can't believe it," he scowled, marking a compass direction on his map. "I'd guess we can get back to our camp by walking at about 110 degrees," he explained, pointing out the direction they'd need to take. Folding his map he tucked it safely back in his vest pocket. "I'd estimate we have about five miles to go, and if we can stay out of that dense underbrush, it's probably about an hours walk as the Crow flies."

"Well let's not fly," Ed chuckled, walking toward their first camp site at Split Rock Falls.

As they walked at a rather fast pace, every so often they'd chase up a deer or some other animal, and the frightened animals would all run about fifty yards and then suddenly stop and turn to see who these strangers were that had invaded their peaceful surroundings.

"It looks like we can have fresh venison if we want," Dave grinned, still hiking at a rather fast pace through this primitive and untouched forest, stopping only to confirm his compass direction from time to time.   As they came closer to the campsite, the brush once again became much thicker, which was a sure sign that they were getting near the Split Rock River.   Finally Dave spotted their tent, which they'd only missed by about a hundred yards, which was a big relief. After a short rest, and lunch, they started the horrible ordeal of repacking and reloading the boat for their short trip to *Hay's Bay*.   Since the wind had picked up and was from the southwest, they would be protected by land almost all the way, so their overloaded boat wasn't in any great danger of capsizing in those larger waves they could see off in the distance in the open waters of the *Sabaskong Bay*.

As they motored along the shoreline, Dave said. "I think we should do some serious fishing tomorrow."

"Fishing," Ed choked. "What are you talking about?"

"Yes fishing," Dave repeated, once again looking at his map. "Just a few miles to the southwest is a small Indian reservation, right on the eastern shore of the open water, and I think we should check that out before we start making any noise looking for gold. I suspect these are the same Indians that chased my fanny out of here last year, and I'd like to see just what's going on at that reservation anyway. Maybe we can see if they really make their living fishing or not, and just how busy they are this time of the year. Once we're aware of their daily routine, we'll stand a far better chance of not being chased by them. If we can prevent any contact with them, it certainly would be to our advantage. Don't you agree?"

Both Ed and Bill stared straight ahead as they thought about what Dave had just said.

"Yes, you're probably right," Bill finally agreed. "But just what is it you'll be trying to find out?"

"Well, if their tribe is netting fish every day, they sure aren't mining gold, and chances are they won't be chasing us off their plantation if they're fishing. If we know when they clean and deliver their fish, or when their cooking, or drying their nets, or whatever they do on weekends and windy or rainy days, we can change our schedule accordingly, can't we?"

"I see what you're saying," Ed smiled. "You know, I love to fish anyway, and I didn't bring these binoculars along for nothing."

Bill was pleased by how well the Islands were protecting them from the wind, as they wove their way from channel to channel, finally reaching the small entrance to *Hay's Bay*. And after a great deal of searching they eventually found a perfect landing spot behind a natural rock cove that completely hid the boat from anyone that might be motoring along that shoreline. Then just above this boat landing, less than a hundred yards from the shore, they found a perfect campsite that was surrounded by tall pines, where they'd be well hidden from view as well as the wind, and it was also very close to their magic stream.

"I believe this is only about a quarter of a mile from where we'll probably start our search for gold," Dave explained.

Just to the southeast of their camp, was a high cliff where they could overlook the entire area and the large peninsula that separated this bay from the much larger open waters to the south. The open water area was so large they could not even see the other side of the lake, and that was where the majority of the Indian netting took place. Although Bill had watched the Indians fish in the *Sabaskong* many times, the winds were far more dangerous there than the steady rolling waves of the larger open water to the south.

After a brief rest, it took much of the remaining day for them to unload and set up their new campsite.

"We'll need to chop some dry fire wood," Dave explained. "And if we use dry wood sparingly, and cook over hot coals, we shouldn't be sending up too many smoke signals. I also suggest we keep our campfires small, so they won't be spotting our fire at night."

"Okay, I'll be your man," Ed snickered. "We sure haven't been getting enough exercise lately," he groaned, as he grabbed his ax and went to search for a good dry tree trunk to chop at.

"Hey Ed, you can use this canvas to cover the wood when your finished," Dave laughingly shouted, tossing a tarp in his direction.

Bill had already started gathering rocks to build a large fireplace that would shield the fire from the wind and hide the flames at night.

"I'd guess we have enough water to last us only a few days," Dave said. "So we'll probably have to fetch some fresh spring water from our aquifer in a few days."

"I bet that spring water is as pure as you'll find anywhere, but just to be on the safe side we should probably use some of our water tablets," Bill explained, placing one large shelf like rock on top of his fireplace.

Later that night, when they were finished with all their chores, they celebrated with some cold beer, and Ed prepared a large sirloin steak with fried potatoes, which they'd brought with them for this very occasion. Then after dinner, they watched the Northern Lights dance across the sky as they visited about how they'd start by first trying to pan for gold. It was very late when they finally crawled into their sleeping bags, and much later in the morning when they finally awoke to the persistent sounds of a woodpecker rapping away on some distant tree.

As they stretched their tired muscles they could see it was going to be another beautiful day, and as Dave poured his freshly brewed coffee they chatted about the beauty of this new paradise they'd found, and how they'd casually catch fish today while they'd watch the Indian's work habits from a distance.

"If we catch some Walleye today, we can probably store the filets in plastic bags in that cold water, rather than pull an ice chest up into the tree every night." Dave explained.

"Oh I forgot to tell you, there's an outpost lodge near Split Rock, where we can buy ice if we need it," Bill said. "They cut lake ice all winter long up here, and bury it under sawdust in their ice sheds where it lasts all summer long. But I agree with you, that cold water will do the trick if we can hide them where a bear won't smell them out."

It was a big relief for Bill to finally be able to open the throttle to full speed, as he followed the channel lines he'd sketched on the map the previous night, marking their route around the peninsula that had protected them from the winds off the open water area to the south. Finally they reached the open water area and Bill slowed the boat so it would better ride the huge rolling swells that were always present on the east side of the lake's vast open water area. Although it was a fairly calm day, they had the advantage of a steady breeze as they angled southeast toward a group of islands that were about a half-mile off shore from the Indian's Canadian Reservation. As they motored around to the inland side of the islands, Ed could easily see across this fairly large bay called *Burnt Harbor*, and as he scanned the shoreline he said, "The Indian's buildings all appear to be located on what looks like a small island right at the mouth of that river."

Once on the more protected inland side of these islands, Bill pulled back on the throttle, while Ed more carefully studied the reservation with his binoculars.

"I can see the mouth of the river," Ed whispered, "and just south of their buildings, there's a bridge that crosses over to the mainland. It looks like they have an old truck parked on that point, just north of the bridge." Pausing a brief moment he continued, "Things look awfully quiet, and I don't see any boats, so they must be out fishing." Then as he stood up he turned toward the open water, scanning the horizon. "And I can't see a single boat out there," he said squinting through his binoculars. "Would they have netting rigs on their boats?" He asked Bill.

"I've seen their boats many times on the *Sabaskong*, and if I remember correctly, they use several types," Bill explained. "They have those flat scows they use when they drop what they call a snare net across a channel, and they use the larger boat, when they drag a net behind them in the deeper water. If I remember correctly, those larger boats have rigs that stick out on both sides."

"Well let's just seriously fish around these islands for a while," Dave said, getting a rig ready for trawling, "and we'll just kind of watch for them to show up somewhere."

"You guys go ahead and fish," Ed said, moving to a more comfortable position at the stern of the boat and swinging his feet up on the side so he was more comfortable. "I'll just study things, until you catch the first fish."

No sooner had Ed said that than Dave screamed, "My God, I just had a huge strike," and then his pole suddenly bent deep under the boat, and as his line spun out rapidly he awkwardly tried to get things under control by pressing his thumb hard against the line on the reel.

"Oh boy," he yelled at the top of his voice, "This baby's a big one!" Awkwardly standing up he tried to change the fish's direction before it used up any more line. Finally he got the fish to turn, while reeling in as fast as he could to try and keep a tight line.

As Bill watched Dave's neck widen with each run, he could see the sweat began to run down his forehead, and after almost twenty minutes of intense battling for control, Dave finally began to take charge, slowly reeling the fish toward the side of the boat. But every time the fish came near, the same raging battle would start all over. Eventually the fish broke the surface, and as it rolled toward the depths, Dave shouted, "My God it's a huge Musky! Get the hook," he yelled.

Dave quickly raised one arm as he desperately tried to wipe the sweat from his left eye, which was now burning from the salty sweat that was obscuring his vision. Finally, after more than a half hour, Dave sneered. "I can feel him weakening," and as the fish rolled closer to the boat, Bill hooked him behind the gill plate as the huge Musky made one last desperate attempt to escape. Not until the fish lay on the deck of the boat did Dave drop his arms to his side, flopping back pooped.

"My God, that's a trophy fish if I've ever seen one." Ed shouted. "It's gotta be close to forty inches long. And probably forty to fifty pounds," he yelled.

"Boy, that's a beauty," Bill added.

"We should probably run over to Wheeler's Point and have it weighed and mounted," Dave whispered, awed by its size. "But you know what? This baby deserves to live after that battle."

Straining to lift the huge Musky to check its weight, Bill nodded saying, "I agree, just look at those horizontal stripes on its sides, the true sign of a Musky."

"Well, I prefer eating Walleye. So let's get this one back in the water, so it can live to battle another day," Dave cried, wiping his brow with his large checkered handkerchief.

As they carefully placed the huge fish back into the water, Dave held its tail, moving it slowly back and forth until the equally exhausted fish was once again ready to swim on its own. Once it realized its ordeal was over, it slowly disappeared into the depths for what would certainly be a well-deserved rest.

By noon, several other boats had stopped to fish this area, and one even went a short ways up the mouth of what Dave had identified as the Grassy River, taking them only a few yards from the Indian reservation. Ed could tell they were all from the American side of the lake, by the numbers on their boats; and as he checked each one he confirmed that none of their passengers appeared to be of Indian heritage. Then after catching a dozen or more small Walleye, Bill decided to motor closer to the bridge. The Indian's brown colored truck looked old and unused, but as they got closer they could see that it had a large platform with wooden boxes that most likely were used to transport their fish. There were also several nets hanging behind the two rustic cabins that stood just in front of a rather dilapidated barn, where several horses were casually picking at an unbundled bail of hay.

Since the fishing was very poor near the bridge, Bill decided to motor back across the harbor, so they wouldn't be seen if the Indians returned early. As Ed once again scanned the horizon, he finally saw two large boats off in the distance, heading directly toward them. As they moved closer, he could see the net rigging, but he could not tell if they had any nets dragging behind them. As they finally entered the channel, Ed counted three men working each boat, and there appeared to be some milk cans and large boxes on each deck, similar to the boxes they'd just seen on the truck. Behind each boat, they were also towing a large flat-scow that was filled with what appeared to be wet gill nets, from the day's fishing. Since the rigging was empty, they'd obviously been using the gill nets, and as they docked, several of the Indians immediately began to load the boxes of fish on the truck as the others stretched out their wet nets on the drying racks. One Indian then loaded what appeared to be several empty milk cans onto a two wheel cart, while his helper hooked up one of the horses to this unusual contraption. Once this was all ready, they both got on the other horse and road bareback into the forest, pulling the horse with the trailer and the empty milk cans behind them.

"Where the hell do you think they're going?" Dave asked, raising both eyebrows.

"I bet their hauling water from that aquifer," Ed whispered, as if it was some kind of secret.

"I bet you're right," Bill replied. "That's about all they could be getting, unless they're going to fill them with gold."

"Well they sure as hell don't have any cows out in the woods and with wolf out there, they aren't going to fill them with milk," Dave quickly chimed in.

As Ed refocused his binoculars on the back yard, he continued to talk in a whisper. "I also see a water pump, so just why do you think they'd be going to the woods to get more water?"

"I don't know," Dave scowled, looking confused by what was going on. "Maybe they do fill them with gold! In any event, we'll have to try and keep tabs on that," he grumbled as he stood up and cast his line toward the shore.

After the truck left with a fresh load of fish, the older Indian secured the boats. "Let me see your binoculars," Dave said, reaching out towards Ed.

"He looks like the Chief, the way he's dressed. That beaded leather head band looks like the very same thing White Cloud wears in the Arrowhead Country. And all that gray hair certainly suggests he has the wisdom to be the Chief." Dave paused. "What does that make, seven of them?"

"That's what I counted." Ed replied.

"And you know what?" Dave whispered. "I didn't recognize any of them as the ones I saw last year. And since we can't follow those two that went into the woods, let's see if we can follow that truck and see if they have someone weighing and filleting those fish for them"

As they motored along the shore, they spotted the old truck every few miles since the road closely followed the shoreline, and then just north of Wheeler's Point they watched them pull up to a fish processing building. Bill had stopped at this same location before to buy fish when fishing was bad, and Dave and Bill decided to get out of the boat and walk a few blocks so they could get a closer look, and perhaps buy a few more Walleye for dinner. As they entered the building it was apparent the same tribe of Indians also operated this processing plant, which had a sign on the front that said *Ojibwe Fish Processing, Inc.* As they watched them unload the day's catch, and weigh the fish it was clear these Indians were deeply involved in the commercial fishing business, which suggested that gold was probably not something these Indians were involved in.

"None of these guys look like the ones that chased me out of the woods last year," Dave whispered to Bill as the Indian clerk wrapped a couple of good size Walleye filets for them. "In fact, the Indians I saw were a much tougher looking group than these guys," Dave explained, as they made their way back towards their boat.

Ed was grinning like a Cheshire cat when they returned, throwing a candy bar at each of them, which he'd purchased in the store near the boat dock.

"While you were gone, I got the whole story from this cute little clerk I bought these candy bars from. There are two reservations where the *Ojibwe* Indians live. The one we've been checking out is where they often stay during the week over the summer months, while they are netting fish, and that's because it's close to their fish processing plant that you just checked out. The other is their *Red Lake Reservation* on the west side of the lake, where they live year round, and they don't do much fishing during the winter when the lake is almost totally frozen over. Sometimes they'll net fish in the open waters in the winter, but that's only if they've had a lean year. The entire tribe of *Ojibwe Indians* lives year round at the

Red Lake Reservation and their Chief is a well respected Indian by the name of Bear Claw."

"I'm confused," Dave yelled over the motor noise as Bill directed the nose of the boat back in the direction of their camp. "These Indians appear to be authentic fishermen, and they don't even look like those guys that wanted to shoot me if I didn't leave right away."

"That's not all I found out," Ed continued. "I told her my friend was a close friend of Chief White Cloud from the Arrowhead country and I wondered if Chief Bear Claw would be interested in meeting my friend."

"You're kidding," Dave grunted.

"She said, he's a very nice man, and almost everyone in Baudette likes him and I'd think he'd love to talk with him."

"I don't know what to think about that," Dave replied. "But I'd like to know more about those two Indians that went into the woods before I try talking to their Chief."

"I think we need to try and follow that trail that those two Indians took earlier with their milk cans and see where it might lead us," Bill interrupted.

"But if we find out their just picking up water, that doesn't tell us much," Dave replied. "I think I'd learn a lot more if I could somehow meet their Chief, and I know he'd be interested in all the problems White Cloud is having with that damned arsenic poisoning and taconite dust that's been finding its way into his tribe's lungs and slowly killing them."

"You know I don't think it was this tribe that chased you out of the woods last year," Ed said, "and maybe the Chief could shed some light on just who did chase you last year," as Bill turned into the channel on the south edge of the *Great Sabaskong*.

"You may be right," Dave nodded as he thought about that. "I could tell him about my government authorized prospecting in that area and my close relationship with White Cloud and outright ask him if it was his tribe that didn't want me in that area."

"That sounds good," Bill interrupted, "and we can talk about that while you cook the two Walleye we just bought for dinner," he grinned.

Chapter 5

    Since gold has been found in almost every state, it supports an old saying: "Gold is where you find it." And although it can sometimes be found in the oddest places, it's usually unwise to search for gold in an area that has not produced a substantial amount of gold in the past. Since gold is more than nineteen times heavier than water, it is said to have a specific gravity of 19.3. That means a quart of gold would weigh 19.3 time as much as a quart of water, and it is twice as heavy as lead. Therefore it will readily fall to the bottom of any stream, and stay in that place until the rains, or snow melt, produce flooding or run-off that causes the currents to move the gold further downstream. How far gold will move downstream is determined by many conditions, but in that gold is heavier than most other materials in the stream, it will move very reluctantly. When it does move, it will most often move in a straight line where there is the least resistance. When it confronts a rock or a low spot, it will stop and fall to the bottom or be caught in a crevice around a rock or boulder. If the stream is fast, the gold may be washed far downstream. Therefore, it's best to search for what might be a hot spot in slow deep pools or in the deep crevices around rocks and boulders, where the water slows, or almost stops. After flood conditions, gold can sometimes be found shining on the bank of the stream, but the real "glory hole," is usually found in deep crevices or deep holes where the water has slowed enough to allow a substantial amount of gold to sink and accumulate.

In measuring the value of gold, you should know that 24 grains of gold equals one pennyweight (dwt), and one troy ounce is equal to 20 dwt, which is 31.104 grams. Twenty-four Karats is 100 percent pure, while 18 Karats is 75 percent pure. Fourteen Karats is 58 percent pure, while 10 karats is 42 percent pure.

Gold can be found by highbanking in the spring, drywashing in the summer and fall, or panning and using metal detection at any other time during the year; but you must remember that the weather can make it pretty nasty in some areas during those winter months.

Highbanking in the spring is best accomplished with a metal detector, and should include even the top layer of any gravel bar, and the bedrock and benches high above the river, where nuggets have often been found. As you move into the stream, the basic equipment needed, is a pan, a sluice box, and/or a metal detector. Motorized equipment for dredging, when permitted, can also be very productive. Commercial mining usually employs water or hydraulic mining and grading of huge amounts of soil for a very disproportionate amount of gold, and is therefore very expensive.

Individuals that desire to search for gold by themselves, can usually pan, sluice, or snipe. When the stream is low, it may not be the best condition for using a sluice, and under those conditions one may wish to wade around with a hand held gold sucker or a metal detector. When the river is high and running cold, it can be dangerous, but a sluice is best used when the stream is moving at a relatively good speed. A sluice is of almost no value in a slow moving stream, or where gold flakes are found in clay, since the clay must be broken up by hand to release the gold flakes or the smaller pieces referred to as flour gold. In this case, a pair of dishwashing gloves can prove very helpful.

Panning is the simplest way of finding flour gold, gold flakes, or nuggets, but it's important you use a pan that has riffles along the bottom to trap the gold. Because gold acts differently, it can be found in the bottom of the pan when gently swirling the water and soil that has been scooped from the stream. Gold doesn't sparkle or glitter because it does not have a crystalline structure, but it does shine in either the sunlight or the shade. A 14" pan that has a gravity trap is best, and a black sand magnet works great when you swirl it around the pan, collecting the metallic black sand on the magnet, while leaving a little color from the small flakes of gold that are caught in the gravity trap.

Using a good fiberglass handled spade, a small hand tool, or wire probe for digging can prove very helpful, in both panning and sluicing. When using a sluice, you may wish to use a 5' sluice that has a black mat that acts as a trap and helps you to see the gold, as you shake and wash the rock and sand down the sluice channel. With the sluice, it's important to have several 5 gallon buckets for the soil and gravel and some small bottles to store the gold flakes. If you don't have a small scale, you may get standard bottles in 2 pennyweight (dwt), ½ ounce, and one ounce or larger sizes. A sniffer bottle can also prove very helpful in picking out the small flakes of gold that you can't get with your finger.

A gas fueled pump that floats on an inflated tube, or an electrical shore pump with a dredging hose, can prove very effective when used with a wet suit and goggles. The smaller gasoline driven types of dredges are most efficient in remote areas involving deep potholes and streams that have large boulders and rocks. A small dredge will easily suck up nuggets that are ¾ of an ounce or larger.

As Dave unpacked their gold mining pans, a metal detector, waders and a wet suit with tank, as well as a dredging pump, they joked about how much gold they'd have to find just to pay for the more than three thousand dollars worth of mining equipment they'd brought with them.

"Hell, we'll need to find a dozen ounces of gold just to get our investment back," Ed smirked, starring at the stack of equipment they'd just hid in a smaller "pup" tent near the spot Dave had found gold the previous summer.

"You can't tell there's a tent in that brush," Dave smirked, as he stepped back to look at how well they'd concealed things near the hot spot he'd been so anxious to check out.

"That's a good place for that stuff," Bill said. "Even if they find it, they'll not be able to tie it to our campsite, which is at least a half mile away."

"Yes, but we still need to know the Indian's schedule well enough so we don't give them a chance to find it." Dave grinned.

"I agree — God, I can't believe we hauled all that stuff in my boat," Bill said, shaking his head from side to side.

"Well, let's try a little panning, before we head back to camp," Dave said, handing out three pans and then slipping on his waders."

After each of them were ready, Dave gave them a quick lesson in panning gold before they wadded into the stream and began to scoop the sandy shallows behind rocks and crevasses and the backwater areas where gold might have accumulated — but to no avail. After a good hour, with no success whatsoever, Dave scowled "I don't believe this! Damn it, I'll dig up this whole area if I have to, to prove my point."

Once again Dave's credibility was at stake, as both Bill and Ed looked suspiciously at him, causing him to snarl and curse,

"Damn it, I'm going to find some gold if it's the last thing I do, come hell or high water."

With that both Bill and Ed burst out laughing, "We believe you Dave, but let's call it a day, no one ever expected this to be easy," Bill smiled as he patted Dave on the shoulder. "As you said, we have nothing but time, and I agree that we really should find out the Indian's schedule before we get in trouble or start using any noisy equipment. And maybe we should take a trip to the Red Lake Reservation, if Bear Claw heads back there this weekend. I know I'd feel better if we knew more about his Ojibwe tribe before we start seriously searching for gold. In fact I even felt uneasy while we were just panning for gold."

"You and me both," Ed added. "Hey, I don't know about you but I need a bath pretty bad, why don't we jump in this refreshing stream before heading back to camp."

"Sounds good to me," Bill said, unzipping the tent and packing their waders and pans neatly inside

"That's a damn good idea," Dave said, quickly undressing and jumping into the water.

After they all cleaned up and were getting dressed, Ed noticed his mosquito bites were no longer itching, and those brutal fly bites were actually gone, but he didn't seriously give it a second thought. The other thing they all noticed was that they all felt invigorated, as if the bath had given them new strength as well as cleaned their bodies for the first time in days. Walking briskly back to camp they talked about how they'd hide their boat near the Indian camp in the morning and try to find that cart trail those two Indians took into the woods with their load of empty milk cans.

Making their way to their boat the next morning, Ed said, "I filled the gas tank at the Rainey River boat dock the other day, so we should have close to a full tank to get to the Grassy River."

"Great," Bill smiled at not having to fill the gas tank. "You did a lot more than we did," he chuckled, unzipping the top to the boat and folded it back on the hull. The weather was perfect, and after a quick run to the Grassy River they found the Indian's fishing boats had already left for the day, and since Ed could see no netting boats on the open water, they decided to land their boat a short distance north of the Indian's reservation and try to pick up the trail those two Indians took with their milk cans the previous day. Taking a southeast direction through the woods they soon crossed the cart path, and it was obvious they'd be able to easily track the hoof and trailer tracks, which went both directions in what was a fairly dense forest of tall Pine trees. Before they got started, Dave once again unfolded his map to check the direction of the path and their magic aquifer, and they matched exactly.

"I bet that's where they went," he said. Then after marking his compass reading toward the aquifer he reached down to pick up a branch and brush away a few footprints they'd already made in the sand. "We'll have to be very careful not to leave any tracks that they can spot," he whispered, feeling like the Indians were already watching them. "That would be a dead give away that someone was checking on them." Then as he tossed the branch far into the woods he added, "It looks like we've got a fairly good hike ahead of us so we better get started since we have to get out of here before they get back, which was close to four o'clock the other day."

After a cautious hike they finally heard that magic sound of the aquifer, and within only moments they were suddenly standing on the same rock shelf, where those two Indians had probably filled their water cans many times without ever leaving any indication that anyone had even been there.

"This water must be awfully damn good," Bill said, "for them to go this far to get a few cans of drinking water. Where I've camped on Miles Bay, which is on the north end of this lake, we had an old fashioned water pump with a hose going down to the bottom of the lake, and that water was drinkable. I just don't understand why they'd go this far to get this spring water."

"That's something I can't figure out either," Ed chimed in. "Maybe they believe it has some sort of weird magical power."

"That's very possible," Dave said, "most of the Indians I've met always have something magical that they believe in. Well, I think we've unraveled the milk can mystery, and now all we have to do is get back before they do."

As they started back Dave explained, "Maybe I should meet with Bear Claw to find out as much as I can without ever letting him know we've found their magic aquifer. Perhaps I could drive to their Red Lake Reservation and tell him of my friendship with Chief White Cloud from the Arrowhead Country. But even more so, I'd like to check if any of them are wearing gold jewelry."

"According to that girl I talked with at Wheeler's Point, several of the fishermen spend the weekend in town while the others go back to the reservation by boat on our side of the boarder, so it wouldn't be a big deal for us to take Saturday off and drive around the lake. That way they wouldn't suspect we're camping near their Canadian reservation, or even fishing on the lake." Ed said.

"I'm not sure the Chief would be comfortable if all three of us barged in on him," Dave replied, "but I think my driving over there would be a real good idea, and I could tell him I was driving through Baudette and heard there was a Chippewa Reservation here, so I decided to stop and say hello. I know

Chief White Cloud would like to hear that I stopped to visit with him."

"I think that's a great idea and you could leave the boat with Stan at Hellier's Resort, where we parked the car. I know Stan would watch my boat while you were gone, and maybe you could tell the Chief how you were authorized to collect mineral samples in the Arrowhead country, and how last year you were assigned to work in the area east of Lake of the Woods. That way you could tell him about that group of Indians that chased you out of there last year, ignoring your government approval from both Canada and the United States," Bill suggested.

That's a damn good idea," Dave said, staring at Bill. "In fact he'd probably like to hear how Chief White Cloud is having so much sickness from those iron and copper minerals on his Cheyenne Reservations, which maybe he's already aware of," Dave explained. "Well that settles it. I'll drive over there Saturday and see if I can't meet with Chief Bear Claw. Maybe he can answer some of our concerns before we start running that noisy pump and seriously start looking for gold."

It was almost three thirty when they got back to their boat, and it looked like every thing was quite at the reservation as they anchored across the bay from the *Grassy River*, where they were going to fish until the fishing boats returned. No sooner did they cast their lines in the water, than Ed announced, "There they are. We sure cut that one close."

After they docked their boats, three of the Indians once again loaded the truck and took off for their fish processing plant at Wheeler's Point, while the others quickly spread the nets on the drying racks and loaded the heavy water cans from the previous day onto one of the boats. Then in only moments they started their motors and immediately took off across the open water.

"Well it looks like their heading home for the weekend without their truck drivers," Ed said, watching the wake from their boats through his binoculars. "Hell, those water cans were sitting on the dock all night, and we could have just checked them out rather than hiking all the way to the pond," he added.

"Yes, but now we know the source, and if they were filled with gold they wouldn't have left them sitting unprotected on the dock," Dave said.

"You know, I bet if you drove to Baudette tonight you could maybe accidentally meet those Indians in some bar and tell them you're a close friend of Chief White Cloud," Ed said. "Wouldn't it be better if the Indians would be the ones that told you about their Red Lake Reservation?"

"Yes, that would be a much better introduction." Dave laughed. "I guess I better get my butt in gear and plan to go to Baudette tonight. Then you can think of me eating a big steak in a restaurant while you eat hot dogs," he smirked, kind of relishing the thought.

"The hell with that," Bill shouted. "We're going with you, and I know exactly where we can get a big steak. They also have a waitress there that is the best waitress I've ever seen. She serves the whole restaurant without any table ever waiting for a thing — and your water glass never goes empty."

"That sounds great," Dave quickly agreed, "but I was kind of looking forward to getting away from you two for a while," he smirked. "Alright, why don't you two check us in at a motel while I go find their beat up truck, and then later we'll all find that restaurant you talk about before it closes?"

Chapter 6

As the great glaciers of North America began to melt, they left in their path thousands of lakes, many of which were carved out of solid granite while leaving a bed of smooth rounded glacier rock and sand on their shorelines. In the spring, these lakes formed thousands of rushing streams from each lake's abundant snow melt. Since Lake of the Woods is located right on the boarder between the United States and Canada, it is shared by the Provinces of Ontario and Manitoba to the north and Minnesota to the south.   This huge lake measures close to sixty miles from its eastern shore at Nestor Falls on the Trans Canadian Highway to the western shore of Buffalo Bay. It also measures another sixty miles from its most northerly shore at Kenora, Canada to its outlet in the south, by the Rainy River at Wheeler's Point in the United States. The Rainy River then flows southeast some two hundred miles to Lake Superior, north of the Arrowhead Country in north eastern Minnesota.

The southern half of Lake of the Woods is composed entirely of open water called Big Traverse Bay with sandy glacier rock shorelines while the entire northern section is made up of islands that are carved out of solid granite rock and are covered with dense forests of tall pine trees. Without a guide or map one could, and many have, become hopelessly lost in this confusing mix of channels that are composed of hundreds of both small and large islands.

There are many Objibwe, Chippewa Indians, throughout Wisconsin, Minnesota, Ontario, Manitoba and Saskathewan, and in Canada these bands of Indians are referred to as First Nations, and each band has a Chief called Ogima or Gima in their language, who's chosen by their respective tribe members. Objibwe can also be correctly referred to as Objibwa, Objibway or Chippiwa, while the tribe members call themselves Annishinaabe. Each tribe is politically independent and has its own independent government, laws, police, and services much like a small country and as a result the Chief will actually form coalitions to address common problems. Most Chiefs are chosen by Tribal Council members, but many Chiefs are chosen from the last Chief's sons, nephews, or son– in-laws. Many of the Indians speak English today, but some still speak in their musical like language, using words like aaniin (ah-neen), which is a friendly greeting, or miigwech (mmee-gwetch), which is "thank you." The Objibwe Indians have many legends and enjoy telling them as important lessons to their children. The western side of Lake of the Woods includes several land grants from both Canada and the United States, which are divided into what are called bands of Indians, each having their own Chief. Bear Claw's band lives on a small reservation in Canada called Reed River Indian Reservation 36 A, on Buffalo Point at the south end of Buffalo Bay, and this same band also owns a much larger reservation that is in the United States on the north side of Buffalo Bay. In addition to this, Canada also granted Bear Claw's band a small reservation to the east of the lake's open water on the Grassy River, which they refer to as their fishing camp.

As Bear Claw's boats approached the landing on the southwest side of Buffalo Bay, all four Indians were very pleased that Big Traverse Bay was calm that day and they did not have to fight the huge waves that normally rolled across the lake from the west. In fact they made good time crossing the lake and were all looking forward to a quiet weekend at home. Bear Claw was particularly tired from fishing with his crewmen all week, which he seldom did, and while several Indians unloaded the magic water and some fresh fish he headed home. As he reached the end of Cherokee Drive he turned south toward the conference center and park on Ojibwa Bay Street where he lived. He knew the Indians that watched over the boat dock would distribute the fish and water equally to those that were anxiously waiting for their arrival and he was looking forward to a well deserved nap.

All the houses in reservation 36 A had been built by a selected coalition of his band, and they were all inexpensive but well built small homes that met each families needs, which was a policy Bear Claw himself put into place. The conference center was where Bear Claw had his small office and where he often held conferences with either some coalition of Indians or their total band if necessary. Since his reservation was totally independent from the others, they could quickly address specific tribal problems or form coalitions to address the more common problems. Each reservation maintained their own police force and established laws that were rigorously enforced, while maintaining all the normal services, just like a small community does. Bear Claw had asked a fishing crewman to set aside one can of water for the children's story hour, which was usually held on Friday evening.

Later that day, as Bear Claw awoke from a sound sleep, he checked the time and decided to go to the park since it was almost time for the children to start arriving for their story hour. Quickly he hurried to get his full Chief's headdress on and a fresh pouch of tobacco, before slipping on his beaded moccasins and deerskin coat that were made for such special occasions.

"My you look powerful tonight, "his wife said, standing at the door to wish him well. "You must have an important message to share with the children this evening."

"Tonight they will drink of the magical water," he said, carefully brushing past her, and ducking his head to protect the beautiful eagle feathers that had been meticulously arranged in perfect order on his headdress. His beaded necklace was also made with each bead carefully selected with infinite care so that it would be quickly recognized as a sign of honor for the Chief they all loved.

As Bear Claw sat down on the log, you could see he looked worn-out, but the children were not looking at his tired face as their eyes closely scanned his moccasins, then his beautiful beaded belt buckle and necklace, and finally the remarkable headdress that only accentuated his wrinkles that portrayed greatness and wisdom. Once again he pounded his pipe on the log, as if the week had never interrupted his previous story.

Although his fatigue was apparent, his booming voice asked, "How many of you dreamed of Majaimanidoog, the dark evil spirit?"

Only a few did not wave their hands, as they all looked scared stiff, but very anxious to hear more.

"How many of you have thought of Nanabozoho, the great spirit full of tricks?

This brought out an explosion of laughter as many wrapped their arms tightly around their legs and rocked back and forth, nodding their heads as they relaxed a bit and smiled at one another.

"How many have thought about the Great Spirit Kitchimanidoo and the magic water you will share with me tonight?

"I did," they all simultaneously yelled, anxiously waving their arm in agreement. Several shouted, "When will we drink this magic water?"

"First you must know more about this magic water, and the promise you must make," he said, while slowly reaming out his pipe and filling it with fresh tobacco. As the children sat silently staring at him, waiting for him to continue, he finally lit a fire stick and bent over and lit the wood that his wife had gathered earlier. Then taking the long fire stick he lit his pipe, blowing huge puffs of smoke straight up into the air. At last he lowered his head and starred at the children.

Do you remember how the Great Spirit Kitchimanidoo used the great gray wolf Ma'iingon to tell my father Chief Black Thunder of the imminent Sioux attack?

"Yes," they all whispered, rocking nervously back and forth.

"Do you remember how this same gray wolf later led them to this magic water, by providing a light in the sky?

Again they all whispered, "Yes!"

As the fire and stars began to take over the night sky, those that were watching from a distance were comforted by the warm glow it presented of the Chief and the children surrounding the fire.

As Bear Claw took a quick puff on his pipe, he once again starred stoically at them. "What I'm going to tell you tonight, you must remember for every moon of your life and you must never share this great secret with anyone other than another Annishinaabe."

As they all nodded in agreement, their faces took on a hallowed acceptance as the Chief quickly nodded his acceptance in return.

"Many of you would not be here tonight if the Great Spirit Kitchimanidoo had not warned my father Chief Black Thunder of that Sioux attack, giving many of your Great Grand Fathers the time to fill their blankest with leaves and brush to make it look like they were sleeping, while they waited in the woods for the Sioux to attack. When Black Thunder saw the great gray wolf Ma'iinganin in his dream he knew it was a sign of love from the Great Spirit Kitchimanidoo for all the Annishinaabe. The Great Spirit also used the Ma'iinganin to lead them to this sacred water that heals — which you will drink tonight."

With this, the Chief pointed at the milk can that had been placed next to him by two tribe members. As the children stared at the shinny water container their faces clearly revealed how anxious they were to taste the magic water.

"Do you also remember how the Great Spirit marked the ground with a huge smoldering rock and then how the steam swirled high into the air like a serpent?

"Yes," they all cried out in unison.

"And how our hunters had to cover their ears until the water finally shot out of the ground as if it had been trapped for many moons, creating this magical stream right before their eyes?"

"Yes," they all shouted in unison.

"Since then, we have had many signs that the Great Spirit Kitchimanidoo meant this stream be used only for the Annishinaabe people, and that is why you must keep what you are hearing from me a secret."

"We will," they all whispered.

"What were these signs," one child yelled out.

"Alright," Bear Claw replied, with a little chuckle as he readjusted his position to get more comfortable "But when I finish telling you of another important sign, which was only one of many, you must promise me you will return to your

homes and go right to sleep after you taste the water that has magically healed so many of our Annishinaabe Indians."

"Yes," they all again quickly promised once again in unison.

Thoughtfully Bear Claw took his hand off of the can of water he was about to open and emptied his pipe against the log, saying, "Well, let me tell you of the first and most important sign, which happened the very same night of the battle. As Black Thunder's hunting party knelt beside the stream to give thanks for what they'd all just witnessed, this great Chief prayed out loud for his tribe of hunters saying, 'Oh Great Spirit, surely you have provided these sacred waters for the Annishinaabe as our Midewiwin [Witch Doctor] to nourish us and protect us and we are eternally grateful that you have chosen us over the Sioux. Therefore we will always protect this sacred ground as your gift to the Annishinaabe, and never reveal the magic power of this water to anyone other than an Annishinaabe Indian.' Then suddenly, before Black Thunder could finish his prayer to the *Great Spirit*, two of his Indian guards interrupted him, nervously explaining they just saw two *Sioux Indians* marking their trail only a short distance away. Quickly Black Thunder signaled for his hunters to follow him into the nearby woods where they could once again hide and wait for the right time to attack these two Sioux warriors."

With that, Bear Claw stood up and walked around the log he'd been sitting on and crouched behind it as he continued telling the story, while the children all huddled closer together as if they too were about to be attack by the Sioux.

"Unknown to Black Thunder, of the three Sioux warriors who had escaped from that morning's battle, one went to get help while the other two had been tracking Black Thunder's hunting party from a distance, leaving marks for other Sioux warriors to follow," Bear Claw said softly as if sharing a secret.

"And it was only minutes before they could hear the Sioux marking their trail, which was getting very close to where Black Thunder and his hunting party were hiding. Then all of a sudden there they were, the two Sioux warriors standing beside the Annishinaabe's magic pool of water. Just as Black Thunder was about to signal another attack, he thought better of that and decided to watch a little longer, just in case there were other Sioux warriors following them. As he watched them he could see that both of the Indians had been wounded and were still bleeding from their earlier battle and in only moments they both undressed and anxiously stepped into the soothing water to bath their wounds. But just as they began to wash the blood from their bodies the swirling pond gradually began to flow faster and stronger until the current was so powerful they had to grasp each other to stay standing."

With that Bear Claw stood up in a panic, reaching out in every direction as if he was a Sioux Warrior, desperately trying to stand while he washed his body.

"Then all of a sudden the center of the pool opened up and a loud sucking noise could be heard as the two terrified Sioux Indians struggled desperately to free themselves from this powerful whirl pool that had somehow surprisingly appeared out of nowhere, and was now pulling them toward this growing hole in the center of the pond. Then when the Sioux could no longer stand they began to hopelessly swim against the current, and after giving out one last blood curtailing scream for help their bodies disappeared into the hole in the center of the pool. As Black Thunder's hunters stood in shock at what had just happened they became even more confused, no longer sure of anything and certainly no longer sure what this was all about. Then as they all silently starred at the pool the whirling hole slowly closed and magically disappeared as if nothing had ever happened. After a moment of complete silence Black Thunder spoke out loudly. 'Surely we have witnessed the power of our Great Spirit Kitchimanidoo who saved us from these Sioux warriors and healed our wounds. And since this is our land, we must always protect the location of this water as our sacred stream — and to do this we shall never tell anyone other than an Annishinaabe Indian of its magical powers or its location."

With that Bear Claw reached over and took the lid off the water can, as his wife passed out paper cups to the children who remained in complete silence, still overwhelmed by what they'd just heard.

"Before I fill your cup, you must say 'I promise,' and be sure not to waste or spill even a drop of this sacred water."

Chapter 7

After Bill, Dave and Ed secured their camp site, the trip to Nestor Falls took almost no time at all and Stan assured Bill his boat would be safe at his dock. Stan had known Bill as a friend who frequently had rented boats from him and his outpost cabin at Miles Bay, which was some twenty miles out on the lake. And even though Bill now owned his own boat, they still remained the best of friends.

As they drove south on the Trans Canadian Highway the setting sun was just starting to show its splendor as they turned west unto highway 11 towards Rainy River where they'd once again cross the border to Baudette. Bill drove right to the Walleye Inn Motel where he'd stayed previously and they all showered and changed clothes before heading out to search for the Indian's platform truck. The streets were fairly crowded for a Friday night, and after driving from one bar to another, Dave scowled.

"Do you think they drove back to the reservation?"

Ed laughed, "If I just worked all week catching fish, I know I'd at least have a couple beers first."

"I agree," Bill said, "Maybe they're still at Wheeler's Point. I bet they don't even drive down to Baudette on a Friday night. Why don't Ed and I go to Rosalie's Restaurant, where I've eaten before, and we'll wait there while you drive up to Wheeler's Point? As we drove by Rosalie's I noticed she's added a lounge and we can wait there while you check out the bars at Wheeler's Point. And then we can all eat together when you get back, or if you don't get back for dinner, Ed and I will wait at the Motel until you do."

"Well, I'm not going to spend the night with those guys, so I'll definitely try to get back before the restaurant closes."

Wheeler's Point had one main street called River Drive and Dave immediately spotted their beat up truck in front of the View Point Saloon. "*Good,*" he thought to himself.

The Saloon was packed with sunburned fishermen and he spotted the three Indians right away at a table close to the bar. Eventually a bar stool right next to them opened up and Dave quickly grabbed it and placed his order for a cold draft beer. As he spun around with a full mug and a big smile he said, "Hey, are you guy's Annishinaabe?" This caught their attention since most Americans called them Chippiwa, and all three carefully looked him over before the bigger Indian replied. "Yes, why do you ask?"

I've worked closely with Chief White Cloud in the Arrowhead Country, and he tells me there are a lot of Obijwa bands living around Lake of the Woods."

This immediately eased the tension, and their faces relaxed a bit. "Yes, that's true," the bigger Indian smiled, still carefully studying him. "Do you speak Annishinaabe?" The Indian asked, still trying to figure out why he wanted to visit with them.

"A little, but most of the tribe members speak English in the area I work, so I don't use it much."

"What do you do?"

"I work for a Canadian and a U.S. copper mining company doing soil surveys," he replied, pausing a moment before continuing. "Because I'm federally authorized to survey White Cloud's reservations we've become close friends and we often visit about all the problems he's having with the copper and iron sickness his people are fighting." This was the hook that caught their attention, and he again paused shaking his head while starring at the floor — waiting for them to take the bait.

This caught their interest, as the bigger Indian finally asked, "Sickness! What are you talking about?"

"You haven't heard about the problems their having? I thought everyone in the United States knew about that!"

"No, we haven't heard a thing," he said, waving his arm for Dave to sit down in the empty chair at their table. "Come sit down and tell us what you're talking about."

With that Dave held out his hand saying, "I'm Dave Olson, I'm staying in Baudette and just drove up to Wheeler's Point to see if I could rent a boat tomorrow. I've got a few days to burn so I thought I'd try catching some Walleye while I was here," he grinned. "Has the fishing been any good?"

After setting his beer on their table, it was obvious he'd caught their interest and they each shook his hand as they introduced themselves. The bigger Indian Aadi [meaning most important] was obviously their spokesman and the one with a nice smile was Madur [meaning a bird]. The shorter and quiet Indian was Chandak [the moon].

"Where are you from?" Aadi asked.

"I live in the Twin Cities."

Aadi rubbed his chin, still a little doubtful as to why Dave had picked them out in this crowded bar. "We're very interested in what you might know about Chief White Cloud's problems, but first let me assure you you'll catch Walleye on Lake of the Woods. Don't you know it's the best Walleye Lake in the world?"

"That's what I wanted to hear, and there's nothing better than a fresh Walleye shore lunch, as far as I'm concerned."

With that they all smiled, nodding at each other, finally accepting Dave as a friendly person just wanting to visit.

"Alright, why don't you tell us what's happening at Chief White Cloud's reservation. We've heard nothing, and I'm sure our Chief would be interested in hearing about any problems White Clouds having," Aadi said.

Dave took a swig of beer before sitting back and revaluating each of them as he spoke. "As you probably know," he explained almost sympathetically, "Many sections of northern Minnesota have vast iron ore deposits, including the entire Arrowhead country. This iron is taken from a taconite aggregate and for many years the Annishinaabe tribes have used flint, copper and iron to make their knives and hatchets as well as many other things. The copper is obtained from a mineral called malaxite, which is heated to 1,100 degrees Fahrenheit by forcing air into the flame and then pouring the melted copper into molds. In doing this, they were totally unaware of the inevitable arsenic poisoning that can occur, and many tribe members became ill and even died from this as a result. In processing iron ore, they also became ill from the dangerous taconite dust that's found its way into their lungs. And as you may know, these small dust fibers cause cancerous tumors in the lungs, which eventually results in death."

Hearing this, their attention was obvious as their eyes remained fixed on Dave, while Chandak, the quiet Indian was noticeably shocked by what he was hearing.

"Now, as White Cloud's band of Indians age, these diseases seem to be taking more lives, and he's currently seeking federal aid to help treat these problems, but there is really very little anyone can do. You see when they crush these granite rocks they create these small asbestos like fibers called taconite tailings that work their way into the tiny alveoli sacs of the lungs, and it's these tiny fibers that are now blamed for so many miner's deaths throughout Minnesota."

Aadi was already thinking Bear Claw could help White Cloud with their magic water, but he said nothing. Instead he asked a question. "Would you be able to meet our Chief and tell him what you've just told us about these terrible things going on at Chief White Cloud's reservation?"

That was the invitation Dave was looking for, and he was amazed at how easy it had been to get them to suggest a meeting with their Chief. Rolling his tongue against the inside of his cheek and looking up at the ceiling Dave slowly nodded his head. "I'd love to meet Chief Bear Claw, but I could only do it in the morning if he'd have the time."

"Just a minute," Aadi said, "I'll be right back." Getting up he walked outside, leaving all three of them wondering where he was going. Then after he finally returned he appeared happy about something, before taking a quick drink of his beer, "Our Chief would be very happy to meet with you in the morning, and he'll be at his office at nine if that's alright with you?"

"I'd consider it a privilege," Dave said, raising his glass to confirm the meeting. "But, you'll have to tell me how to get there."

With that Aadi waved at the waitress, asking for a paper and pencil to write directions for Dave, while adding, "It's less than an hour drive from here, and I'll tell him you'll be there at nine."

Although Dave was anxious to get back to Baudette, he visited for a while longer before finally saying good night, and heading back to Rosalie's Restaurant for dinner.

"I have a meeting with the Chief at nine in the morning," Dave grinned at Ed and Bill, as they moved from the lounge to their dinner table.

The drive to Red River Indian Reservation 36 A, on Buffalo Point took longer than Dave had planned. Turning on

Cherokee Drive he drove south to the conference center, which was easy to find on a circle like drive called Ojibwa Bay Street. He was just a few minutes late and hurrying inside he found the chief waiting to greet him.

"Aaniin" [a friendly greeting] Dave said as he reached out to shake the Chief's hand. "I'm sorry I'm late, but I made a few wrong turns."

Chief Bear Claw just smiled, pointing at a Chair for Dave to sit down. Miigwech [thank you], Dave replied.

I prefer we speak in English the chief said annunciating each word perfectly, while smiling to let Dave know he was not offended by his attempt to speak Annishinaabe. Dave was surprised at what a large man he was since he'd only seen him from a distance before and his deep wrinkled weather beaten face clearly demanded respect, as Dave sat quietly, courteously waiting for him to speak first.

"Aadi tells me you are a friend of Chief White Cloud, who has been a close friend of mine for many moons. He tells me you have met with him through your work, and have discussed some serious problems his band is having from their copper and iron ore mining they've done in the past. Would you tell me how you first came to know Chief White Cloud?"

"Chief Bear Claw," Dave replied respectfully, "I'm a surveyor for a large international copper mining company, which has hired me to analyze soil samples for copper in many of the wilderness areas in Canada and the United States. I have federal authorization from both countries to do this even on your private Indian reservations, but I feel it is important to meet with each Chief before I start testing the soil on their reservation. And this is how Chief White Cloud and I have become friends."

"Tell me about some of the problems Chief White Cloud is having."

After Dave repeated what he'd told the Indians the previous night he said, "Well there's not much else to tell you other than the long term affects of working with copper and iron ore have had and continue to be a serious problem for his band as they age and grow older. And although the government is trying to help, there is very little that can be done."

"Have you worked with any other Chiefs that I might be acquainted with?"

"Not yet, but I have worked in many non reservation areas in both the U.S. and Canada."

"Do you plan to do these surveys on any of my reservations?"

"Not right now, but I did work in the Caliper Lake area last year, which is right next to your Big Grassy River Indian Reserve 35 G, and I had a serious problem with a group of Indians who threatened to kill me if I didn't leave the area immediately."

With this the Chief frowned and tightened his jaw, starring stoically back at Dave, while pursing his lips tightly in thought.

"I can assure you it was not any member of my band of Indians," he said, and as he thought a moment as to what he might tell Dave next he stammered a bit but continued. "We've had many skirmishes with the Sioux Indians in that area, who have never recognized our reservation boundaries, and it may well have been these same Sioux that ignored your rights. They have tried to claim our lands for many moons and we have a history of countless battles with them. They've also been battling the United States for as long as I can remember, completely disregarding any government control or authorization."

"I'm sure that was probably what happened, because I've never seen an Annishinaabe Indian behave that way before," Dave replied.

After a long conversation they took a brief tour of the reservation, but Dave could see the Chief's mind was bothered by what he'd heard, and after Dave left Chief Bear Claw immediately phoned Chief White Cloud to tell him of the magic water the Great Spirit Kitchimanidoo had blessed them with.

It was almost noon when Dave arrived back in Baudette.

"Well, I'm almost certain it was not an Annishinaabe Indian party that threatened me last year, and we can be assured this band of Annishinaabe has not been mining any gold. In fact they're living as austere as any band I've ever seen. Chief Bear Claw told me the Sioux war parties are a constant threat and they ignore any reservation boundaries and both the Canadian and United State's governments as well. So I believe that's who they were, and based on what the Chief told me, I think we really need to figure out what we're going to do if these Sioux show up again. And maybe those Sioux do know there's gold in our magic river, but I'm almost certain the Annishinaabe haven't found that out yet."

"How many Indians threatened you last year," Bill asked.

"Four — and they were damned tough looking Indians."

"Did they have guns?" Ed asked.

"I'm not sure — and I was so scarred they were going to kill me I just grabbed my belongings and got the hell out of there. I know they had knives, and my guess is they probably had guns also and they were going to use them."

"Do you think you gained Chief Bear Claw's friendship," Bill asked.

"Absolutely, in fact he said if I go back to that area I have his approval to take samples from any of his reservations, and he'd also be very interested in hearing about what I find."

"So you feel comfortable surveying 35G?" Ed asked.

"Absolutely, this guy is a warm human being and I'd trust anywhere."

After they each ordered the biggest steak they had on the menu, they watched the waitress serve every single person in the restaurant without anyone waiting even a minute, and as soon as their steaks were ready they were placed in front of them sizzling hot. As they each ravenously devoured their dinners down to the last morsel not a word was spoken. Then after they ate their dessert they headed back to the motel where they finally went to sleep in a comfortable bed for the first time since they'd left home.

By the time they reached their camp, Dave had checked his map and determined that their camp sight and the magic river were actually not located on Chief Bear Claw's reservation, and that his previous written authorization and his gun were more than enough credential to threaten the Sioux Indians if they gave them anymore trouble.

"Now that I have someone with me I'll remind those damned Sioux of our confrontation a year ago and threaten to have them arrested if they try to chase us off the property again," Dave snarled. Then as he thought a moment he continued. "Would you be willing to use your gun if we had to?"

"You damn right," both Bill and Ed answered simultaneously.

"Alright, let's go to work tomorrow and start looking for gold." Dave grinned, picking out three good size Walleye fillets for dinner and shaking them in a plastic bag of flour, salt and breadcrumbs. While Ed lit the fire, Bill opened three cold beers so they could toast a successful trip to Baudette, while they discussed their strategy for finding gold in their magic stream the next day.

Bear Claw's phone call was quick and to the point after he told Chief White Cloud of the great battle his father had with the Sioux Warriors. "I'm bringing you some water from our magic healing spring, which the Great Spirit Kitchimanidoo has blessed us with. It has healed many Annishinaabe Indians and maybe it will help restore the health of your Objibwa band in the Arrowhead Country."

Chapter 8

"Let's start close to the camp and work our way toward the magic pool," Dave said. "This way we'll be able to find out if any gold has moved down stream. And if we start finding something we'd better have a good place to hide it, because we really don't know what these Sioux Indians are capable of."

Their storage tent had not been bothered during their absence and all their equipment was in tact, but since they decided to start their search downstream they had to carry the gas and their pump and the dredging hose a good quarter of a mile back towards camp. Dave was eager to put on his wet suit and goggles and hook up the air tank so he could start dredging the bottom of the stream, while Ed had agreed to run the sluice box. Bill put on a pair of hip boots and grabbed the metal detector and a pan so he could both wade in the stream and walk the shore to do some high banking or panning in spots that looked hopeful. Their overall plan was to move up stream from the soil they disturbed until they reached the magic pond.

As Dave filled the dredging pump with gas he told Ed, "I'll help you move the sluice box and buckets as we work our way upstream."

"I can handle that," Ed laughed, "you just keep sucking up those big gold nuggets from those potholes, and you won't have to even come up for air."

After the first hour the three of them had thoroughly covered an area as long as a football field without any success. Finally a very disgruntled Dave shut off the noisy pump and sat down on the bank. "If there were gold flakes or flour gold in this stream we should have easily found something by now," he grumbled, drawing in a deep breath of fresh air after breathing tank air for almost a full hour.

"I agree, and I can't believe this aquifer produced only gold nuggets." Bill growled, equally discouraged. "And damn it, for all we know, maybe those Sioux Indians have picked the stream clean."

"Well we've got allot of stream between here and the pond left to cover, and nobody ever thought we'd find gold everywhere we looked just because Dave happened to accidently sit on some nuggets last year," Ed smiled, trying to lift their spirits. "Look guys, we've only been at this for one hour, and we've got a good week's worth of work ahead of us," he chuckled. "So let's get back to work."

As the Objibwa fishing party prepared to leave early Monday for their week of fishing, Bear Claw explained to each crew member how he was going to take some magic water to Chief White Cloud in the Arrowhead Country, and therefore he wouldn't go with them this week. He'd already phoned Madur and Chandak, telling them to buy several large milk cans in Baudette and then drive back to the Grassy River Reservation and fill them with magic water. Aadi drove back to reservation 35 in a rental van to pick up Chief Bear Claw, and take him to White Cloud's reservation with the Great Spirit of Kitchimanidoo's magic water.

"It will take us about three to four hours to reach Chief White Cloud's reservation," Aadi said, as they arrived at their Grassy River reservation, where Madur and Chandak were waiting to load the magic water into the van.

"Chief, we need to tell you we heard a strange noise while we were at the magic pond. It sounded like a motor boat, but we don't think it was."

"Do you think it was on our reservation?"

"I don't think so," Madur said. "It was more downstream to the north, kind of off in the distance. Then right after we finished loading the water, it stopped, but we've never heard a noise like that near the pond before."

"If you hear it again I want you to go and find out what it is."

"Yes Chief," they both nodded as Bear Claw hurriedly climbed into the van.

"Thank you so much," Bear Claw said to Madur and Chandak as he and Aidi left for the Arrowhead Country.

The sun was just setting as Chief Bear Claw and Aadi arrived that evening at White Cloud's Reservation. Bear Claw had never been there before and he was impressed with the well established buildings and the cleanliness of things. Although he'd met White Cloud many times, he'd forgotten what a powerful looking Chief he was, but he could also tell he was very troubled by the problems Dave had shared with him earlier.

"You must be hungry," White Cloud said, pointing the way to his home where his wife was waiting to serve dinner.

"I've heard of the many battles you've had with the fearsome Sioux warriors in the past, just as we've had, but I was never aware of the magic water you speak of. Does this water really heal as you say?" White Cloud asked, excited by a possible answer to the many sicknesses his band was plagued with.

"We've seen it heal wounds many times after our battles with the Sioux," Bear Claw replied. "And we think it also keeps our band healthy, so we often drink it in place of lake water. However, we also know it only helps those

Annishinaabe Objibwa Indians who've been selected by the Great Spirit Kitchimanidoo, and we must ask the Great Spirit to bless your band if they are to benefit from this miraculous healing water. I'm convinced the Great Spirit created this water to also help us defeat the Sioux warriors when my father Black Thunder asked for his help. As I've told you over the phone, this same pond sucked the two Sioux warriors into the earth when they sought its help in cleansing their wounds."

"I pray he will help us," White Cloud said, as he starred toward the heavens. "May I ask you to lead our Tribe in a prayer to the Great Spirit Kitchimanidoo tonight?" White Cloud asked as his wife placed their dinner on the table.

"Tonight we will become one large Tribe of Annishinaabe in prayer to the Great Spirit, but you must first show Kitchimanidoo those Objibwa Indians who are suffering from these illnesses."

With that, White Cloud asked his wife to send a message to the entire Tribe for such a meeting that night.

By the time they finished eating the sun had disappeared and they could only see the huge fire that was surrounded by White Cloud's entire Tribe of Objibwa Indians as they walked to the meeting place. As both Chiefs moved to the center of this gathering it was an awesome site to see, and after White Cloud raised one hand for silence, even Mother Nature and all the sounds of the night became silent.

"Tonight we will call upon the Great Spirit Kitchimanidoo to help fight the many illnesses our Tribe has been fighting for so many moons. Those that have been plagued with these illnesses have not been able to solve this problem, and tonight Chief Bear Claw will share a secret his band of Objibwa Indians has known for many moons. But what he is about to tell you must be kept as an Annishinaabe secret. This is because the Great Spirit Kitchimanidoo once blessed Chief

Black Thunder's warriors when he sought his help to destroy the fierce Sioux warriors that were about to attack his hunting party. But before we pray to the Great Spirit Kitchimanidoo, I ask that all those that have an affliction come forward and sit in the front where the Great Spirit can see them."

Approximately fifty Objibwa Indians stepped forward as Chief Bear Claw in his full head dress studied them closely before he shared the miraculous story he'd recently told to the children of his own band. There was complete silence as he spoke and finally he described how the two Sioux warriors were sucked into the center of this magic pool of water.

"We have had many injuries and illnesses healed since then, and tonight we will pray to the Great Spirit Kitchimanidoo to bless the water we've brought you from this magic pool so that it might cure your sick Annishinaabe Indians who are in need of help.

As Bear Claw reached up toward the sky his powerful voice echoed in the night.

"Oh Great Spirit, may we call upon you to grant us another miracle for Chief White Cloud's band of Annishinaabe Indians. We thank you for protecting our hunters from the Sioux warriors and the healing of their injuries. We thank you for the healing water that flows from the ground and we ask that you let it heal these sick and disabled Annishinaabes that sit here before you tonight."

With that the entire group reached toward the sky shouting, *"Miigwech Oh Great Spirit,"* many weeping as they prayed for his help. Others shouted *Miigwech Chief Bear Claw* as he bowed his head in prayer.

"We all thank you Chief Bear Claw," White Cloud whispered, "and we will distribute this miraculous water to our sick and disabled with the hope that the Great Spirit of Kitchimanidoo will share your blessing with us."

That evening Chief Bear Claw couldn't help but think of the many sick Annishinaabe Indians, while Aadi silently drove him back to their reservation.

I can only hope this blessed water will help, Bear Claw thought to himself — knowing it could be months or even years before any sign of a cure might be reported back to him.

On the second day of searching for gold, Dave and Bill had persuaded Ed to try the wet suit, and Bill agreed to operate the sluice box. This way they would each get some hands on experience with the various methods of searching out gold. After the first hour they'd still found nothing, and they were seriously beginning to doubt if they'd ever find gold. Then suddenly Madur and Chandak walked out of the woods, walking right up to Dave and asking him what he was doing there. Dave was as shocked at seeing them as they were of seeing him, but he recovered quickly.

"I'm doing the work I didn't finish last year he explained. After talking with Chief Bear Claw, he told me I was chased out of here last year by Sioux Indians, so I decided to delay my trip to Banff and finish the mineral search I didn't accomplish last year. Your chief gave me his approval to also work on your land, but I don't think I'll be able to do that this trip — but I'll certainly call him before I do," Dave explained.

Ed and Bill just stood back in amazement over how tactfully Dave had handled what could well have become a very serious problem.

Although they accepted his response, they were still concerned asking, "Why do you search the water to get your minerals?" Madur asked.

"Oh, that's the best way since minerals flow downstream carrying the soil from so many other areas." Quickly changing the subject he added, "But I'm still worried about the Sioux chasing me out of here again, so I hired these two government officials to help me should they try to kill me again. This is Canadian property and I have government approval to work here, and this time I'll have them arrested if they give me any more trouble. God you scared me, when I first saw you, I didn't recognize you and I thought you were the Sioux."

Finally they both laughed as they shook his hand, accepting everything he was telling them as fact.

"Yes, the Sioux are fearless warriors that totally ignore our rights as well as the government. And you do need to be very cautious of these Sioux. Both Sitting Bull and Crazy Horse were Lakota Sioux that became great warriors and as you know the Lakota's have withdrawn from the many treaties they'd once signed with the United States over some one hundred and fifty years ago," Madur explained.

"Are those the same Indians that say they are no longer citizens of the United States and had that big battle at Wounded Knee?" Dave asked.

"Yes," Chandak replied, "they've actually denounced their citizenship, asking all Indians in their area to join them. Lakota country actually includes Nebraska, North and South Dakota, Montana, Wyoming and Minnesota, and there are three bands called Lakota, Nakota and Dakota, with the Lakota always giving us the most trouble."

Chandak seemed well versed in Sioux history and he went on to briefly tell Dave about their big battle with the Sioux many moons ago, which created a permanent problem between the Annishinaabe Indians and the Sioux.

"It seems we're always fighting to hold on to our reservations, while they completely ignore anything the governments of both Canada and the United States say," Madur went on to explain. "They believe all government treaties are just worthless words on worthless paper, and they intend to run their own lives, ignoring all laws that are set by any other government than their own."

"I'd be careful of them if you see them again," Chandak added. "We told Chief Bear Claw we were hearing noises in the forest, and he told us to find out what they were, so that's why we came here. He will be pleased by what we tell him, because these Sioux present a constant problem to us also."

"Yes, be careful," Madur cautioned. "In fact there's a sizable band of Sioux living just to the north of here, right between Miles Bay and the Sioux Narrows, and they often hunt in this area."

With that they abruptly turned and left, leaving as quickly as they came.

"Say hello to Chief Bear Claw and tell him I'll be in touch with him when I find time to work on his reservation," Dave yelled, as the two Indians noiselessly disappeared into the woods.

Not knowing that Chief Bear Claw had already traveled to see the Annishinaabe Indians in the Arrowhead Country, Dave said. "I thought these guys would be fishing today, I wonder what changed their schedule?"

"What they said about the Sioux scares the hell out of me," Bill said, "and as I said before, maybe those Sioux have picked this place clean since you last saw them."

"That could be." Dave said thoughtfully staring into the woods where the two Indians had just disappeared.

"Hell, maybe we should go find this Sioux band and see if they're selling any gold trinkets," Ed laughed.

"That's not a bad idea," Bill agreed.

With that Dave stood up and defiantly said, "Alright lets go up stream and see if there are any nuggets left. If we can't find any today, I'd like to find that damned band of Indians who've violated the mineral rights for both country's, and teach them a thing or two."

Ed laughed. "So what's good for the Goose is good for the Gander! Eh! — How about, first come, first serve?"

That evening they sat by the fire talking for several hours.

"Why don't we head over to Nestor Falls in the morning and see what Stan knows about the Sioux Indians in this area. I bet he knows every thing that goes on up here, and maybe he can shed some light on what these Sioux do for a living," Bill said, knowing Stan would surely have some information they might be able to use.

"That's not a bad idea, but we don't dare tell him what we're really doing here, or we'll have a gold rush on our hands," Dave grinned, poking a stick at the few remaining embers still glowing in the dark.

"You got to find gold before you can have a gold rush," Ed chuckled, heading for the tent.

Sitting down with Stan for a good restaurant breakfast the next morning, he explained that a sizable Sioux band had been living at the Sioux Narrows for many years, and they often worked for him, guiding inexperienced fishermen on Lake of the Woods.

"Their really a very hard working band of Indians and many have homes and jobs at the Sioux Narrows. There are a few rebels that still live out on the islands that do some crazy things now and then, but I believe most of them are good Canadian citizens."

"I saw a Totem Pole on an island near Miles Bay when I stayed at your outpost cabin," Bill said. "Would that belong to some of the rebels you speak of?"

"Oh yah, that's close to where they have their camp sight. In fact, these guys live like they did a hundred years ago. They make their own canoes and live in teepees, just like they did before any Canadians settled in this area. Why do you ask?"

With that Dave told him of his confrontation with the Sioux in the Caliper Lake area last year, while he was searching for mineral deposits for that Canadian mining company.

"We're camping close to where they chased me out of the woods last year, and we're worried they might try it again. I know they scared the hell out of me when they threatened to kill me, and they meant business even though I was authorized to be their. I guess that's why Bill thought we should visit with you."

"Well I can't speak for that bunch of Indians that live in the woods, but the ones I know would never do anything like that," Stan said.

"What do these rebels do for a living?" Bill asked.

"They live off the land, hunting and fishing as far as I know. Some of them come in here now and then, but I seldom see them."

"Do they have any money?" Ed asked.

"Oh sure, but they only buy beer or tobacco when they come in here."

Stan kind of smirked, pausing a moment. Then he laughed, "You know, one time they tried to sell me some jewelry they'd made, but I told them I had a distributor from Vancouver that takes care of that end of my business. Actually it wasn't that bad looking."

"So you didn't buy any?" Bill asked.

"Oh no, I told them to talk to my distributor, and maybe he could help them."

"Do you know if they did?"

"Yes, if I recall correctly, I think they did."

"What kind of jewelry did they make?" Ed Asked.

"Just a moment," Stan said, walking back to his office. When he returned, he laid a large discolored metal band on the table, which had several ornate Indian carvings in what was a crudely hammered out piece of grayish looking metal. "I bought this from them because I felt bad that I was unable to sell their jewelry, but it's really kind of different, don't you think?"

"Yes it is," Dave said, trying to fit it on his wrist. "I can see why you didn't try to sell their jewelry. I bet you paid them a pot full of money for this?"

Stan Chuckled. "Yah - I paid ten dollars, which they turned around and bought a case of Labatt beer with."

"So you were the good Samaritan eh?" Ed laughed. "Hell I'd pay you ten dollars for it, just as a collector's item."

"You got yourself a deal," Stan said, pushing the jewelry towards him and glad to get his money back.

On their way back to camp, Dave closely studied the dark colored band and the stick figures that were crudely carved in it. Clearly it was made from a heavy metal and the surface was very slippery, which prompted him to take out his knife and scrape the surface. "My God, there's gold in them there hills he shouted," staring at a swatch of clean gold under the contaminated surface of the band.

Holding out the jewelry for Bill and Ed to see, they both stared at it — shocked.

Finally Ed shouted, "That's the best deal I've ever made."

What do you think they covered that gold with?" Bill shouted over the noise of the motor.

"I'll be damned if I know, but we now know they've found gold in our magic stream."

Chapter 9

Gold is resistant to natural chemicals and acids, and it does not tarnish and cannot be destroyed. Getting gold wet or leaving it exposed to the elements will not damage it and it will remain bright and shiny forever; however, gold is never found entirely pure in nature and is often alloyed with silver, platinum, copper, or coated with mercury, which creates a bright silver color and requires a trained individual to remove the mercury. Gold is also very malleable, which allows it to be flattened or reshaped and it will not shatter when pounded.

Dave, Ed and Bill were all very discouraged that the Sioux were apparently aware of Dave's find and that they'd probably been watching him very closely before they chased him out of the woods last year.

"So that's why they threatened to kill me," Dave said, chocking down a hotdog for dinner. "I was the only legally authorized person that could remove minerals from this government property and they had no legal right to any gold find whatsoever. Sure I had to meet government requirements, but my finds were mine to keep if I desired, and my agreement clearly stated that."

"Are you sure of that?" Ed asked.

"You damned right I am," Dave scowled. "That's one of the reasons I agreed to risk my life in the north woods for these mining companies. But I never expected to find gold, and gold wasn't what these companies were looking for in the first place. They wanted copper!"

"Okay," Bill interrupted, "So what are we going to do now?"

"Hell, they aren't supposed to trespass on government property or steal gold. I was legally authorized to search that area and I struck gold and it's mine."

"But that was last year, what about now?" Ed asked.

"My contract is still in effect, and that's still my claim."

"Alright, I hear you, but what can we do about it?" Bill asked again.

"Well let's take our guns and go get our gold from those Sioux Indians."

"And how are we going to do that," Bill asked.

"We'll find their damned camp and take our gold back," Dave yelled.

Dave had been an all star guard at McAllister College and you could tell his dander was up and he was ready for a fight.

"Don't you think there's a better approach? Ed kind of chuckled, waiting for Dave to rethink what he'd just said.

"I agree," Bill interrupted, "and I think we could find a better way to do this than go in there with our guns blazing," as he tried to calm Dave down and talk seriously about some other strategy that might work.

"First we'd have to find their camp if we followed Dave's suggestion and then find out just how many Indians we're dealing with, don't you think?" Ed asked.

"Sure," Dave finally conceded, but he was still visibly upset.

"I think we should go and make one last search for gold before we do anything," Bill suggested, still trying to calm things a bit. Then finally after much bantering back and forth they all agreed that Bill was right, and they decided to spend the rest of the day searching the stream near the magic pond, before they went after any Indians.

The hike to the pond was far more difficult than they anticipated with Ed trying to juggle the sluice box under one arm and their pump under the other with the dredging hose continuously slipping off his shoulder. Dave carried the air tank on his back and a full tank of gas and the metal detector, while Bill's back pack was filled with a wet suit, and a pair of hip boots. He also carried the shovels and several gold pans under each arm as they hiked toward the pond. As soon as they reached a location that was just downstream from the magic pond, Bill began dredging behind the larger rocks in each backwater area while Ed operated the sluice. Since the shoreline seldom flooded because it was fed by an aquifer, Dave decided to ignore any high banking and before he really got started panning he reached down and picked up what appeared to be a gold nugget.

"Hell yes he shouted!" so loud that Bill had to come up from under the water and see what was going on.

"Maybe those Damned Sioux didn't get all the gold after all," Dave hollered."

Both Ed and Bill hurried over to inspect his find and grinned at the gold nugget reflecting the sun like a star in the night.

"You've gotta be kidding," Ed yelled out, "and no body's going to take this one from you," he shouted, pulling out his gun and waving it in the air. Then after throwing his gun on the ground he ran toward the magic pond and jump in clothes and all, splashing water in every direction. As Dave grabbed the gold nugget tightly in his hand he started to follow Ed but stopped abruptly when he noticed the pool of water was suddenly swirling in an all encompassing movement around the outer edge of the pond. As Bill cautiously moved closer he yelled, "Ed get out of that water!"— but to no avail, as Ed was almost instantly swept into the powerful current that was now uncontrollably pulling him around the outer edge of the pond. Then abruptly there was a loud sucking noise as they watched Ed's arms flailing powerlessly in every direction, finally disappearing into what was now a large swirling whirlpool. And then just as quickly as it had started the sucking noise stopped and the entire pond was sucked into the ground right before their eyes, leaving an empty hole where only moments before the aquifer was bubbling up a steady flow of crystal clear water. As Bill and Dave stood paralyzed by what they'd just seen, they watched the last remnants of the stream slowly vanish, leaving only a few puddles of water where they'd just started their search for gold.

Dave finally shouted, "My God what's going on?"

"What about Ed?" Bill screamed, looking toward Dave who was still frozen in place, gawking at the empty hole in the ground where Ed had just disappeared. As they both stood starring in shock, neither one spoke as the eerie silence became so overwhelming that it took several moments before they turned to look at each other, realizing that they had to do something immediately if there was any possibility of saving Ed's life.

Then suddenly, like a cry in the wilderness, a distant voice yelled out, "Will you get me the hell out of here?"

Taking a deep breath Dave and Bill yelled simultaneously, "You damn right," as they ran toward the granite ledge where the Indians had filled their milk cans with water and starred down at a gaping hole that resembled the mouth of a monster. Just across the hole to nowhere, was a huge metallic like rock resting on the bottom of what was once the pond. Then in an effort to see where Ed's voice came from, they both glanced along the crevices around the side of this huge rock, finally recognizing a mud covered body and Ed's panic stricken face helplessly glaring up at them while clinging to a handle like root that had obviously saved him from being washed further down the hole to eternity.

Within moments Dave turned and ran back to the pump that was still sputtering loudly and removed the dredging hose, which he dragged behind him as he raced back to where Ed was trapped, and nervously clinging to that root for dear life. Attaching his belt through a metal eyelet that was on the end of the hose he hurled it down to Ed shouting for him to wrap that belt under his arms and around his body so they could pull him up to safety. Awkwardly Ed maneuvered the belt around his chest with one hand while he cautiously fastened the buckle with the same hand before he finally let go of the root he'd been clinging to and slowly wrapped both arms tightly around the small dredging hose, carefully maintaining his balance in the slippery mud so he wouldn't slide into what could well be an endless pit to hell. Then after what seemed like an eternity to Bill and Dave he finally shouted. "Okay, I'm ready."

Both Dave and Bill slipped and fell several times before they at long last dragged Ed over the edge of the rock where they all laid breathless and totally bushed. The shock of everything that had just taken place left all three of them speechless as they silently prayed, thanking the power above for the miracle that had obviously just saved Ed's life. Once they regained their senses, and began to think normally, they looked hopelessly at the equipment they'd carried to the pond and realized most of it would be worthless without any water.

"Perhaps we can use the metal detector, but the rest of this equipment is useless," Dave growled, shrugging his shoulders in disgust, while walking casually over to shut off the noisy pump that had only been adding to their bewilderment.

"Let's get the hell out of here," Ed said, still partly in shock and completely worn out by what he'd just been through.

"Ed, why don't you just sit there and rest while we hide this equipment somewhere," Bill said, patting him on the shoulder. "We sure as hell aren't going to carry it back to our hideout now — then after we get back to camp we can try to figure out this whole damned thing and what we do next."

Once again there was complete silence as they walked toward camp, both happy on one hand, and obviously depressed by the unbelievable things that had so shockingly changed almost everything in just a matter of minutes. Here it was almost lunch time and their magic stream had just completely disappeared right before their eyes, and they had no idea what that meant. But they were also damn happy Ed was walking back to camp with them, even though he was covered with mud and didn't look or feel anything like his usual spirited self.

After washing up a bit and having lunch and a nap, Ed felt much better as Dave started a fire to make dinner, while Bill thoughtfully sat quietly and watched the sap sputter as the flames engulfed each pine log, snapping noisily. Finally Bill asked, "Just what the hell are we going to do now?"

"I don't have a clue," Dave cried out just as if he'd been waiting for someone to ask. "In fact this whole damned trip has been a complete disaster as far as I'm concerned, and I'm ready to give it all up right now."

"Hey," Ed shouted right back, with his same old spirited attitude. "I'm feeling much better, and I'm thinking we're just getting started. Hell Dave, you just found a nugget and now I can finally believe in you for the first time. And now you're saying you want to quit? Bullshit! Let's go into town and buy some metal detectors and a couple shovels and get serious."

Both Bill and Dave stared at Ed and then suddenly began to snicker.

"Hell, we came up here to find gold and now that you found some you want to give up?" Ed repeated, raising both arms in the air as if Dave was an idiot.

With that both Bill and Dave broke up laughing, Dave falling to the ground and rolling over and over at his ridiculous suggestion to go home.

"I guess that doesn't make a lot of sense, does it?" Dave laughed as he slowly got up, shaking his head and brushing the dirt off his clothes. "Hey, while these coals are getting ready for cooking and we can no longer swim in the stream, I'm going to take a quick dip in the lake and get some of this mud off of me. Anyone care to join me?" He yelled.

"Hell yes, Bill said, while Ed took a rain check saying, "I've had my swim for the day. I'll just stay her and watch the fire."

In the morning, they took the boat down the Rainy River all the way to Baudette, where they picked up two more metal detectors and a couple more shovels and were back at camp before noon.

"You know, ever since Stan told us about those rebels that live on the island, I've been thinking about that Totem Pole I accidently saw in the wilderness near Miles Bay," Bill said. "And since it's too late to start looking for gold today, why don't we take the rest of the day off and go and see it, and maybe we can spot that Sioux camp Stan told us about. Then we can spend the whole day looking for gold tomorrow," he added.

"If we do that, we better take our guns with us," Ed replied, looking forward to a different type of adventure than he'd just experienced the previous day.

"That's a damned good idea," Dave chuckled, "I've been thinking the same thing, but I didn't have the heart to say so - I thought you'd think I was nuts."

"Dave, get your map out and we'll head across the *Sabaskong* and look things over. We probably wouldn't find gold slipping around in that mud today anyway, and don't you think we should probably let the stream bed dry up a bit before we go back to work," Bill explained.

"I agree. I certainly didn't feel like digging in mud today," Ed said, grabbing his holster and strapping it on tightly.

While crossing the *Sabaskong,* Dave noticed on the map that there was an Indian reservation just a couple miles north of where Bill said he'd seen that Totem Pole.

"I bet those rebels are living on that wilderness reservation," Bill said. "It's funny, but I've fished all around that reservation and never realized it was there, and I bet I looked at my map at least a hundred times."

The *Sabaskong Bay* was very tame that day as they crossed the open water in almost no time at all.

"We're only a short distance away from that totem pole," Bill yelled over the motor as they sped wide open between two tall granite cliffs that stood almost a hundred feet above them. "We'll be able to see it when we reach the open water just ahead," he shouted.

Then as they came out of the narrows the sun once again came into view just as Bill turned sharply between a small round shaped island and the shoreline.

"There it is," Bill shouted, pointing at a twenty foot totem pole that was shinning in the sunlight as if it had planned to greet them with its scary faces of eagles, bears and what looked like Witch Doctors.

"My God, I'd never have believed this if I didn't see it," Ed said almost reverently. "That's worth the whole trip — it's amazing!"

As they drifted slowly to shore Dave jumped out with the anchor and secured the boat before he looked up and studied the art work more closely. "No, I wouldn't have believed it either if I hadn't seen it," he whispered respectfully. "I can't believe the same guys that chased me out of the woods would be capable of making something like this."

Chapter 10

Totem poles are carved from tall mature trees, representing the emblem of their family band, and they often serves as a marker at the entrance of their home, honoring the ancestors or a particular band and their standing, rights or accomplishments, or as a memorable ceremony or record of a spiritual experience. It can also serve as a symbol of a band's exploits, experiences or qualities. In all cases it tells a story that can be only revealed by the one who knows the meaning of the various animals, fish, birds and designs; all related to where they are placed on the pole. Since some bands claim to be descended from certain figures it can also symbolize an important or historical story that is somehow concealed within the art work of the totem pole by its owner and carver. Since totem poles serve as emblems, they are seldom worshipped as Gods. They only represent bands of Indians or clans and attempt to tell a story through some unusual combination of various animals, fish, birds and designs.

The Eagle is thought to be the strongest of creature because it has such huge wings and such sharp eyes, which rule the sky and control all the men and creatures below him. He is thought to have caused storms and made lightning with only the snap of his beak, and because his wings often sound like thunder, he's called the thunder bird, a powerful and mystical leader.

The Raven also ranks high on the totem, also over seeing all man and creatures below, and because of his strong beak he is thought to be feared by both creatures and man. He is also the guardian of both creation and knowledge serving as the provider.

The Wolf is very crafty and cunning, and because he moves mostly at night he's seldom seen by man. He often attacks and steals food and is very competitive with both man and other creatures. He's known for his intelligence and leadership and has a strong sense of family.

The Bear should not be tampered with or provoked since it is believed he has the ability to change from animal to man and back again. The Bear also has the ability to give birth.

The Beaver can be friendly, but when provoked can cause flooding or dig traps for man in lakes, streams and rivers, causing either men or creatures to drown or become trapped.

Mosquitoes with their long blood sucking nose and large eyes can see in the dark, and therefore they've become a nuisance to both man and creatures alike. It is believed they also have the ability to take away wealth and therefore are feared by man.

As Bill, Dave and Ed stood enthralled, while staring up at the tall totem pole, a brisk wind suddenly swirled sand in every direction.

"Bill, I'd have never even seen this if you hadn't taken us right up to the shoreline — it blends in perfectly," Ed whispered in respect for the totem poles unique but somewhat scary carvings.

"I know," Bill replied, "I just happened to be trolling for Walleye between that island and this shoreline, or I'd never have known it was here."

"You know it's hard for me to believe the Sioux Indians carved this," Dave said in a much softer voice, like maybe the Sioux were already watching them. "I've seen a few totem poles carved by the Ojibwe Indians that look somewhat similar, but this isn't anything even close to what I'd expect from the nomadic Sioux. Maybe the Dakotas Sioux would try something like this but they don't have big trees out there."

"Dave, I've stayed at the Sioux Narrows at a place called Totem Lodge and I've seen some very interesting totem poles there. Since Stan told us a Sioux band lives in the Narrows and perhaps on this island we're standing on, they may have followed the custom of other tribes by now and maybe they're no longer so nomadic," Bill explained. "And they sure as hell have the trees to carve on up here. But because of their nomadic history, I doubt if they could move their Totem poles to all the places they go. And Dave's right, in the Dakotas there are no tall trees, other than in the Black Hills."

"Well it may well be that the rebels on this island did chop down a tall pine and place it here," Ed said, still whispering. "But I agree with Dave, I've seen some art work by Karl Bodmer that would scare the bejeebes out of you. They show nothing but slender poles decorated with painted animal skins and human skulls covered with branches and feathers. Yuk!"

"Well let's get back in the boat and try to circle this big island and see if we can spot their canoes or any sign of life." Bill said. "I've taken enough pictures of this thing and we can try to figure out what it means when we get back to camp." I'm also a little worried about the wind that's just kicked up because we don't want to try and cross the *Sabaskong* in ten foot waves."

As they motored north toward *Obabikon Bay* they realized that there was no passage around the north side of what the map showed to be an island, and Bill quickly turned around to return to camp the way they came once he realized the land he was trying to circle wasn't really an island. As they made their way back through the tall cliff passage they could see that the *Sabaskong* was much rougher than when they crossed it earlier, and Bill slowed the motor to study the situation before attempting to head out into what appeared to be some very large waves.

"This is exactly what I told you about, but since we're not too heavily weighted down let's at least give it a try," Bill yelled over the gusting wind and the motor noise.

Slowly moving out into the open water, the huge waves seemed to be pushing them along until the crest of a huge wave moved under them and the boat dropped a good five feet. Knowing it would be much tougher to turn back against these waves if they stayed on this course much longer Bill made a quick decision to turn around while they still could.

"I'm sorry, but with these huge waves, rocks can appear out of nowhere and we'd better go back and wait it out on the safe side of the *Sabaskong*. It's just getting too dangerous to be out here now, and these waves seem to be getting worse every minute," Bill shouted, slowly starting to turn the boat around while everyone hung on for dear life. As the boat crested sideways in the waves they were all heavily drenched with water before they were turned enough to finally hit each wave head on. Then as Bill finally increased his speed into the wind the bow of the boat would rise up almost perpendicular before it suddenly dropped in its wake, still showering them until they finally reached the protection of the tall cliffs that quickly calmed both the wind and the water. Once they were safe they looked back at the wild *Sabaskong* and they could see the waves were now getting much larger. Soaking wet, and with the bailing pump running wide open, they headed toward the Totem Pole area, where they could camp until things settled down. Just a short distance north of the Totem Pole, Bill found a sandy beach where he decided to beach the boat, and since they were now far more protected from the wind because of those tall cliffs, it appeared to be an ideal place where they could build a fire and dry out a bit before the sun went down. At the end of the beach was an outcropping of solid granite that had a shelf like indentation in the rock, making an ideal fireplace about waist high, and Dave immediately started building a fire since they might be there for a while. On each side of the inboard motor were two cushioned seats, one hiding a reserve ten gallon gas tank and the other providing a storage space that Bill started to search — finding a small pup tent, an un-inflated air mattress, a first aid kit and thermos with water still in it, and some matches and a few cooking utensils all efficiently folded together in a tight package.   As the fire reflected its heat off the rock wall their clothes dried quickly and Ed suggested he try and catch a few walleye for dinner before the sun set. Later, after Ed cleaned three small Walleye he finally got to drink a beer by the fire while Dave cooked the filet in that small frying pan. Since the wind did not seem to be letting up, Bill raised the top to the boat and folded the two side seats into beds as the evening chill took over and the sun sank below the tall cliffs to the west.   Dave inflated the air mattress and set up the pup tent on the beach, where he decided to sleep until the wind would once again let them safely cross the big *Sabaskong Bay*.

Chapter 11

Dave rolled and tossed uncomfortably in his pup tent because his mind kept telling him he should sneak out alone and try to find that Sioux Indian Camp. Maybe he could find out if they had his gold and steal some of it back he was foolishly thinking. Several times he tried to forget that ridiculous idea but each time he rolled over to sleep, the same thought would return. Finally he stood up and fastened his gun tightly to his waist and quietly made his way toward the Totem Pole. The full moon was just beginning to climb high enough above the horizon so he could maybe find a trail that he would take him closer to their camp. As he followed one of the more heavily used trails he checked his compass several times to confirm his direction. He realized that walking only by moonlight in an unknown forest was really stupid, but his adventurous spirit seemed to throw all caution to the wind, which was still gusting heavily from time to time. As a safety measure he finally decided to draw his gun from its holster and carry it in his hand if he happened to annoy a sleeping bear or some other dangerous creature. Then after walking what seemed like a mile or more and having second thoughts about the wisdom of what he was doing, he finally found himself standing next to several birch bark canoes, all turned upside down to prevent them from filling with rainwater. As the moon reflected off the bottom surface of each canoe he could see they were beautifully built handmade canoes, made with the utmost of care. *My God, the art of building birch bark canoes was lost years ago,* he thought to himself. *If these guys are carving totem poles and building birch bark canoes, they can't be all bad. I remember how I felt sorry for the Sioux when they fought the government for their freedom at Wounded Knee, South Dakota.*

As Dave continued toward what was hopefully their camp, he began to hear noises off in the distance and he decided to move off the trail and follow his compass to be on the safe side. Every so often he'd hear a dog or a distant voice and finally after walking only a short distance further he saw the glow of a campfire through the trees. Slowly creeping closer he could see several tops of teepees with their supporting poles protruding from the top, forming the chimney hole for smoke to vent from what were obviously there homes. *I can't believe they're still living in teepees*, he thought. As he cautiously crawled to a safer location so he could better observe what was going, he could see maybe a dozen or more Indians sitting around a very large fire, which was reflecting brilliantly off their teepees.

Sitting quietly and observing the peacefulness and sheer joy of their family gathering was something Dave would never forget. Here was a tribe of Indians that had cast aside the luxuries of today's world, living peacefully and obviously independently with Mother Nature in this remote area of the Canadian wilderness. *Maybe humankind could learn something from this when we someday evaluate all the damage our profit seeking monetary system has wrought on our human race,* as he sat stunned by what he was actually observing first hand. Not only was the camp well kept and clean, the peacefulness was infectious as Dave's emotions took over. *How in the world could I even think of walking in there with my gun and demanding the gold they once owned before the Canadian Government stole it all from them?* In fact the thought of taking anything from them turned his stomach, as he slowly turned and shamefully crept noiselessly away, embarrassed by the fact that he had observed such a private moment without them knowing they were being watched. That shame and guilt followed him all the way back to his tent, and since the wind had finally relented he decided to wake Bill and Ed so they could all return safely to their own campsite under the light of what was now a brilliant full moon.

The return trip was uneventful this time and the surface of the *Sabaskong Bay* was almost mirror like as they sped southeast toward *Hay's Bay*. After reaching their camp site a little past midnight, they slept hard until that damned woodpecker began his usual noisemaking ritual the next morning. During breakfast, Dave finally decided to share his secret venture to the Sioux camp, vowing that whatever those Indians had found in gold was theirs to keep, while suggesting that the three of them continue to find whatever gold they could before they'd pack up and head home.

"If I hear you right," Ed responded, "you've had a change in attitude regarding those Rebels - am I right?"

"You got that right. What I saw last night has changed my whole life!" Dave said, in an almost prayerful tone. "My God, these people are the most valuable type of humans I've ever seen. Not only are they living completely independent of our societal greed, they are at peace with themselves. The only thing they are doing that doesn't conform to our wishes is that they are still fighting for their right to an independent life and the land they once owned. In fact, that damned gold once belonged to them, long before Canada and our country took it all away from them. And what really shocked me is these people are truly living off the land, and they appear much happier than we'll ever be." Dave explained, his eye's actually tearing up a bit as he talked.

"I hear you," Ed said, as Bill nodded, staring thoughtfully at Dave.

"So where do we go from here?" Bill asked, still looking at Dave for an answer.

"I don't think it changes anything," Dave said, "but I sure as hell don't plan to take anything from them or go in there with our guns blazing."

"So where do we start look for gold?" Bill asked.

"I have some thoughts on that," Dave said, biting at the inside of his lower lip as he stoically stared at both of them.

"Well why don't you spit it out so we can agree or not!" Ed smiled, pushing his glasses up on his forehead.

"Alright, here is what I'm thinking. When I stood on that rock where those Indians filled their water cans and looked down into that hole that seemed to reach down to the center of the earth, I could still hear rushing water. I've never been one to crawl through underground caves, but if we could get down there we might find an underground stream or cave and more gold than we ever hoped for."

"I agree with that!" Bill said nodding his head up and down in support of what Dave was saying. "In fact I've been thinking the same thing."

Ed starred at Dave and Bill as if they had just lost their mind. Letting out a loud whistle and razing both eyebrows he smirked in disgust. "You know at times I've thought you guys were nuts, but now I'm absolutely sure of it."

"Now let me finish," Dave raised one hand to stop Ed from interrupting again. "Since gold sinks to the bottom of the stream and if this piece of gold I found really did come from the Rockies — then it's highly unlikely that most of it found its way up here to our magic stream, and the real mother load is

103

not up here, but down in that aquifer. If we took one of our fishing poles and dropped a line down that gaping hole we could get an idea of the distance down to the aquifer, and then we could perhaps determine if it was even possible for us to get down there or not." After taking a quick breath he continued. "And if we can't get down there, we'd probably have better results if we first dug around this huge peculiar looking rock before we started looking in that dried clay bed of our magic stream."

"You know, while Dave was sneaking up on the Sioux last night," Bill paused, "I was thinking about all the crazy things that have been happening to us lately, and all these strange things are finally starting to make sense to me. If you remember last winter, most of the ski resorts in the Rockies closed early because of the lack of snow. And yesterday, when Ed decided to jump in the pond and the stream suddenly decided to disappear, I felt it was because the spring snow melt no longer had the same power to force that water and gold up to our stream. And since our magic stream has been crystal clear, I believe the water is coming from the mountains and not the lake. But that would mean our aquifer has to flow under *The Lake of the Woods*."

As Dave starred at his map, he slowly nodded his head, fully agreeing with Bill. "I think you're absolutely right! And if it's coming from the Rockies it has to be going under the lake, because we're on the eastern shore and it couldn't come from anywhere else. In fact, if I drew a line parallel to the direction the Rainy River flows, it would take us from this hole in the ground right under Chief Gray Cloud's Reservation at Buffalo Bay."

"Well you can be assured that I'm not going down in that hole again," Ed growled.

"No, and I wouldn't expect you to," Bill said. "But you guys know I've done some mountain climbing and I've also been in a few difficult caves over my lifetime. I'm not saying it wouldn't be tricky to get down there, and I also understand it could be very difficult without the right equipment."

"Yah! So now we're going to make another investment?" Ed scoffed.

"Well I've got this gold nugget to help us with that," Dave grinned, holding it up so they could see it reflect in the sun light. "But first let's get an idea of just how deep this aquifer is and if it's even feasible to try and get down there. I'll get my fishing pole and tie a lead sinker on the end of my line and lets go see if this is just a pipe dream or not," Dave said, excited by what they might find.

Grabbing some sandwiches they all headed toward the dried-up pond, anticipating that this just might prove successful, even though they could feel Ed's usual enthusiasm was missing.

Standing on the rock shelf, they could see the hole was at least ten or twelve feet across and Dave reached out with his pole so the line would drop dead center, hoping it would make a straight drop down to the water, which they could all hear very clearly now.

"Boy, you're going to need some flashlights down there," Ed said, still doubting that anyone in their right mind would want to venture down into what looked like a hole to hell.

Dropping the sinker seemed to take forever as Dave slowly let the line run out, and as it dropped further and further without being impeded in any way it was obvious the line would soon reach bottom on the first try.

"There it is," Dave shouted, bouncing the sinker on what sounded like solid rock rather than water. Quickly he marked his line by tying a knot in it. Handing Ed the pole, he asked

Bill to hold the line at the knot while he hurriedly walked backwards until the line stretched out some fifty feet from Bill.

"We're in luck," Bill said, with a big grin. "It looks like we could drop a rope straight down to that rock bottom without any interference at all. Doesn't it?"

"Hell, we should be able to see down that far with my flash light," Dave said lying on his stomach and flashing a light down into the hole, as Ed rushed over to grab hold of his feet. "In fact I think I can just make out a rock bottom like cave down there. But I can't see any water."

"Well I can sure hear it," Bill said, "so it's gotta be there somewhere."

"I bet that was solid granite my sinker hit down there," Dave explained.

"Yah — and that would explain things even more." Bill said, still trying to sort out his thoughts. "I bet the aquifer runs under a solid layer of granite rock, and that's why the lake water hasn't contaminated it — they're separated by a solid layer of granite."

"Hell, I bet this aquifer could run all the way to Lake Superior, like the Rainy River, and the only reason it formed this pond in the first place is because this huge meteorite like rock ruptured the crust of the earth, so now when the aquifer is under pressure it forces water up to the surface and forms our magic stream," Dave explained, still a little doubtful that they'd truly figured this whole miraculous phenomenon out just yet.

Chapter 12

The ice age is often referred to as the glacial age, which resulted in the presence of huge polar ice sheets in the northern and southern hemispheres. These Glacial stages in North America left widespread impact on the landscape, suggesting the Great Lakes were carved by the ice age. Most of the lakes in Canada, Minnesota and Wisconsin were also gouged out by these glaciers and later filled with glacial melt water. The most recent glacial period peaked approximately 20,000 years ago, when extensive ice sheets lay over a large part of North America, and although the last glacial period ended more than 8,000 years ago, its effects can still be felt today from this moving ice that carved out the landscape while creating erratic land formations. It was also thought that the weight of the ice sheets was so great that they cracked the Earth's crust and mantle, allowing aquifers fed by glacial melt to develop under the earth's outer crust.

Once many of the great glaciers of North America began to melt, they left in their path thousands of Canadian Lake beds that were carved in solid granite, while others rested on a bed of smooth rounded glacier rock. In the spring, these Lakes would also overflow from snowmelt, which formed thousands of rushing streams and tributaries such as the Rainy River and even the great Mississippi River

The western slopes of the Rocky Mountains provide the largest watershed in the world, emptying its snow and glacier melt into the Pacific Ocean; while on the eastern slopes of the

Rockies, all the way from Jasper to Banff in Alberta Canada, the same type of watershed occurs, continually filling thousands of lakes and streams across Canada and all the way to Lake Superior. Many large underground aquifers have also been fed by this mountain runoff, of which a countless number still remain hidden and unknown to man.

In the years 2001 and 2002 Alberta and Saskatchewan, Canada experienced severe drought conditions, plunging the Great Lakes to their lowest level in thirty years. A reduction in both snow melt and rain caused these conditions, often drying up streams and kettle lakes as well as severely reducing the flow in many of our underground aquifers. Worse yet, these drought conditions have continued to increase, and now there is considerable evidence that over the last 100 years, the increases in human activity, especially the burning of fossil fuels, has caused an accelerating increase in atmospheric greenhouse gases, which trap the sun's heat. As a result, the consensus theory of the scientific community is that this greenhouse effect is a principal cause of the increase in global warming, which is a growing concern and believed to be a chief contributor to the accelerated melting of the glaciers and polar ice.

"You remember I told you about the Rocky Mountain ski lodges closing last year," Bill explained. "That's because they hadn't had enough snow, and I believe our aquifer has lost so much water pressure that it suddenly dried up our stream."

"I agree," Dave said, thoughtfully taking a bite of his sandwich and trying to decide what to do next.

As they thought about making the necessary changes in their plans it was obvious that Bill had to be the one to risk his life because he was the only one who'd done some cave and mountain climbing, but they also knew that they'd need to take every precaution in that one mistake could prove to be fatal.

"You're probably right, that it won't be that difficult for Bill to climb down there," Ed finally replied, "but my close call makes me think we should probably give up while we're still ahead. Just searching around that big rock and the river bed, would satisfy me."

"Well that may well be what we end up doing," Dave agreed, looking directly at Ed, "but let's at least discuss lowering one of us down about fifty feet to check things out if it can be done safely. If we're finding gold up here, there just could be a chance that there's a mother-load of gold down there just waiting for us. Bill, in that you've done a few caves before, what do you think your chances would be at getting down there safely?"

"Well, if we have the right equipment, there's really not that much to it," Bill explained. "Yet I can understand Ed's concern because of what was clearly a very close call for him — but you have to remember that was the result of a very unusual situation, where the aquifer's water pressure suddenly disappeared and sucked him down without any warning. And if that were to be reversed, let's say the pressure suddenly returned, a life vest would handle that if I was attached to a rope, and you couldn't pull me out of there fast enough as far as I'm concerned. At least I wouldn't be sucked into the earth like Ed was. To be very honest I just don't think it would be a problem to go down there and look around."

"So what equipment do we need that we don't already have?" Ed asked.

"I think we have a couple options," Bill explained. The first could be that I use the less complex repelling equipment that we could buy, while the more complex system would be to use a locking hand winch or a heavy duty hoist with sixty feet of wire cable or climbing rope. We could even build a wood frame like they use for window washers on tall buildings if we had to, but I'd suggest we just strap a rope to that tree over there and I use the repelling equipment. In any event, I'd like to study the walls of that hole before I decide which system would work best. It would be much easier to repel myself down there if the wall's mostly rock. And if that's the case, pulling myself back up would also be much easier. However, if the walls aren't stable it may require that we do build a frame to hold a cranking or power type winch to raise me up and down. We could also build a center frame using the pine trees we have here, but we'd need to rent or buy a good power winch or cranking system somewhere." As he thought about it for a moment more he continued. "Or, even a three tier pulley could do the job. Of course my preference would be a well mounted battery driven winch." As he paused to think about that.

"That all sounds pretty far-fetched to me," Ed said, still not buying in on the idea.

"Come on Ed, where is that old spirit you had, before that aquifer scared the hell out of you?" Dave laughed. "Damn it, I agree with what Bill's saying, and I bet we can find just about anything we need in Baudette."

"Well before we head back to camp let me check out the walls of that hole, to see if I could repel myself down there," Bill said, grabbing Dave's flashlight and walking toward the granite ledge overlooking the aquifer."

As they all stood on the rock cliff Bill said, "I think I'm going to have to get on that meteorite and look down from over there," he explained, walking around the empty pond and jumping several feet onto the huge meteorite. As he stared down at the rock surface of the meteorite he cautiously reached down and touched its surface. "God this is strange looking stuff, it feels like metal but it's porous, like it's been heated to a very high temperature. In fact it looks almost like lava." Then as he finally walked to the edge near the hole he lay down on his stomach and flashed the light across the hole, carefully studying the side of the cliff, all the way to the bottom.

"Dave, from here it looks solid but why don't' you put a heavy weight on that fish line and bounce it off that wall, and I'll watch if it loosens any soil as you bounce it down to the bottom."

As Dave bounced a fairly large rock he'd tied to the fish line, Bill yelled, "*Eureka*, I think I can repel down there all the way, it appears to be solid granite right to the bottom."

Hiking back to camp, they were all excited, even Ed had relaxed a bit and was talking enthusiastically about what they might do to help lower Bill down safely into that scary hole.

That evening Bill made a list of everything they'd need to help him repel down to the aquifer, with just some basic mountain climbing gear. The only problem was Baudette would be a difficult place to find mountain climbing gear, but they could probably improvise by buying comparable equipment at a local hardware store.

"We should also be able to find some winches or pulleys at an auto supply shop, but clearly repelling down that wall would be by far the easiest way," Bill said before drifting off to sleep.

"This is the best block and tackle system available for the price," the clerk explained. "And you could also attach this pulley system if you'd like. The price includes 100 feet of 1/2 nylon double braid rope that weighs only five pounds, and has a breaking strength of 7,400 pounds — so it can lift almost anything you need to lift. It would also make a great block and tackle system with a 5-1 pull advantage if you use this four inch pulley. In fact this pulley will get most jobs done at a fraction of the cost of a winch."

"Would you have anything that we could hang this on like they have for a well?" Dave asked.

The clerk looked surprised as he thought for a moment. "Well, yes I have an old used rotating arm with a manual winch out in back that you might be able to use. Why don't we go look at it and see what you think."

"That sound interesting, let's take a look at it," Bill said.

The winch appeared old but was still functional.

Dave looked at Bill and whispered, "Couldn't we somehow fix that stand to the base of that tree and extend the swinging arm out over the edge? It looks just about the right length so we could easily crank things up if we had to."

"That would be perfect," Bill replied, turning to ask the clerk, "Would you be willing to rent that at a reasonable price for a few weeks if we buy the stuff we just looked at?"

"Yes, I think we could do that."

After getting another hundred feet of rope and a half dozen pails, a tree strap, a safety belt, several pairs of leather gloves and hook attachments, the clerk finally said, "Hell, I'll let you use that winch for ten bucks if you bring it back undamaged. We haven't had any use for it since I've been here anyway."

The trip back to camp went well once they figured out how that extension arm on the winch best fit in the boat so it wasn't banging against the boat with every wave.

Then after installing the rotating winch against the trunk of the tree they spent the rest of the day preparing for Bill's descent down into the aquifer the next morning.

Dave was up at the crack of dawn fixing a good size breakfast as Ed nervously paced back and forth while Bill kept rolling and tossing in his sleeping bag, obviously thinking and dreaming about his climb down into the aquifer.

At the pond, Bill tied one end of the rope securely to the tree strap and then pulled the rope tight as he walked to the edge of the cliff where he gave several tugs to tighten the knot before threading the full hundred feet of rope through a hook on his safety belt. Then he tested it by leaning fearlessly over the edge of the cliff. Next he wound the rope around his left leg and up across his back, anchoring it under his left arm pit before he grasped the rope tightly with both gloved hands and once more jerked it taught before he leaned backward over the edge of the cliff. Then without any warning he just pushed off into space, sliding down the rope several feet before both feet made contact with the wall. As Dave and Ed watched nervously, he slide effortlessly down the rope, his feet making contact with the solid stone wall about every ten feet and in almost no time at all he was standing safely looking up from the bottom of that dark hole.

"I'm okay," his voice echoed through the cavernous cave as he turned on his flashlight to study the surging stream that was rushing past him just a few feet from where he'd landed. As his flashlight searched the washed out cavern wall he was amazed at its size and he could see a good twenty feet downstream before the water disappeared into a smaller cavern like hole. He stood only a few feet from where the water entered the cave which was much larger than he'd anticipated. At the widest part of the stream it was only about ten feet across to the other side, and although it appeared deep in spots he could see bottom in many areas where he might risk crossing to the other side. As he studied the size of the cave he concluded it was perhaps twenty by fifty feet in overall dimensions with the ceiling no more than six to eight feet high at the tallest point. He could also see boulders with a lot of sand on both the upstream and downstream side, which meant he'd need some buckets and a small shovel. And to be on the safe side he yelled for them to also send down a life vest and his plastic jacket, which he was anxious to put on because the chill and humidity was overwhelming — which he hadn't anticipated. While they lowered all the things he asked for, he studied the shallow water and was shocked to see what appeared to be gold nuggets stuck in crevice after crevice as well as behind several large boulders.

My God, there's got to be millions of dollars worth of gold here, he whispered.

"What does it look like Dave yelled?"

"I'll tell you when I get back up there, in the mean time I'm going to be sending up some buckets of sand, as quick as I can, in that it's colder than hell down here, and I'll have to work fast."

Pulling down enough rope so he could move freely he grabbed the first bucket and began filling it with the nuggets he could see and in only a short time he had it half full. Setting that bucket aside he next began to hurriedly fill one bucket after another with the sand that was trapped around the boulders and within a half hour he had all five buckets ready to be hoisted up on the winch. In that he could send up three full pails at a time, the entire task was accomplished in less than an hour and a half, and after that Bill hurriedly began his climb back to the top, first attaching the bucket filled with nuggets to the end of his coiled climbing rope. Although the wall was slippery from all the moisture the ragged edges formed perfect foot holds as he slowly worked his way back toward the light at the top, finally working up enough of a sweat that it stopped his shaking from the cold and eerie damp place he was very glad to be leaving. After he finally reached the top, both Dave and Ed helped pull him back to safety where he sat exhausted but smiling like he had a huge secret to share.

"I want you to pull up my climbing rope, but very carefully, it just may have our entire future hanging on the end."

The excitement was infectious as both Dave and Ed cautiously lifted the one remaining bucket to the top and then starred dumbfounded at what was in it.

"You've gotta be kidding," Ed screamed, as Dave tried to quite him down, shocked by what they were both gawking at in disbelief.

"We've got to get this stuff out of here fast," Bill whispered, "we don't dare have someone walk out of the woods and see this."

Ed pulled his gun and said, "they'd have to stare this down first."

"Needless to say, we need to hide this safely just as quickly as we can, and I'm sure we're going to find even more gold flakes and flour gold when I go down there again — and you guys still need to run all this sand through the sluice today"

Quickly they unstrapped the hoist and hid everything that would even suggest anyone had ever been there as they hurriedly carried all six very heavy buckets back to camp, where Ed and Dave set up the sluice in a protected area by the lake.

In the meantime Bill packed the nuggets in small bags and hid them under the plastic gun-wale of the boat, where only his long arm could reach them. This way they'd be able to cross the border on the lake in their boat without any check point, and then trailer the boat at Baudette, after someone drove the car and trailer there from Nestor Falls.

As Ed operated the Sluice, Dave finally finished feeding all five buckets of sand, reclaiming another five full bags of what was almost certainly high grade gold flakes and flour gold. After Bill showed them where he hid the nuggets he also added the five bags, while Ed and Dave returned the sluice to a safe hiding place. Then after grabbing a beer they finally all took a deep breath and began the celebration that lasted well into the night before they all collapsed from exhaustion, now very happy that they'd listened to Dave's unbelievable story a year ago.

The next day was almost a repeat of the previous day, all dwindling off to a few small amounts of flour gold the eighth day, when it began to rain so hard they couldn't leave the tent for two whole days. In fact, they'd found so much gold they could no longer hide it in the boat so they slept with it, with their guns close by. After the rain finally stopped, they hid all the equipment in their pup tent, where it was highly unlikely anyone would ever find it, since they had no room for it in the boat — sadly recalling how they'd tediously hauled it to their first campsite on that memorable boat trip to the mosquitoes infested Split Rock river. They had no idea when or if they'd ever come back here, but they were almost sure that the equipment would be safely waiting there if they did. The next morning they stashed the rest of the gold under the boat seats leaving some in bags out in the open on the bow of the boat, with the hope no Game Warden would stop them. In fact, there was just too much gold to hide anymore. Ed had agreed to drive the car to Wheeler's Point, and after a quick trip to Nestor Falls, Bill thanked Stan for all his help before he and Dave returned to the camp site to pick up that large winch they had agreed to return. As they were carrying the winch to the boat, Dave suddenly stopped saying, "listen!" — Gradually lowering his end of the winch to the ground he yelled, "I hear that damned stream running again."

With that, Bill dropped the other end of the winch, and they both ran toward the stream. With each step the noise became louder and louder, and then suddenly there it was, just as if it had never stopped running at all.

"My God," Bill yelled, "I'm glad I wasn't down in that hell hole when the water started up again. I bet it's because of all that rain we had!"

"Bill, we could of come up here a hundred times and never experienced what we've seen happen here. That window of time for all this to happen was no more than a couple weeks."

"You got that right, and I don't think we'd of found much gold in the stream, if that was the only place we'd been able to search."

As they stared at the stream rushing by them they knew that someone or something had been guiding them, for this was far more than just a coincidence.

Bowing their heads, they both felt certain there had been some form of *"Devine"* intervention, and for some unknown reason they'd clearly been blessed, even though they weren't sure as to why.

Finally Dave Spoke. "I'm going to see that these Indians in the Arrowhead country benefit from our success," he whispered. "And although the Indian's at the Sioux Narrows probably don't want any financial help, we should also do something for them to help regain the freedom they once enjoyed on what was once their land."

"I agree," Bill said, nodding his head, "but even though we now have the gold in our possession, we've still have a long way to go before we know for sure just what we do have."

"You're right, who knows, maybe we just found some fool's gold and think we're rich, but I'm sure glad Bear Claw has his magic stream back. In fact I think we should tell him what we experienced with the stream, and what the draught in the mountains created while we were working here. Maybe we can even help him find that same aquifer on his reservation."

"Dave, I've wanted to tell you that I think you're right about that aquifer running under the lake, but I don't think we should tell him or anyone about the gold."

"Oh I agree, but let's go see him while we're still up here," Dave said. "It would only take us a couple of hours, and I'm sure he'd respect us for telling him what happened at the stream. And you know, if they did dig a well he'd not have to cart all those water cans back and forth"

As they finally left their beautiful camp site, perhaps for the last time, they could feel the bonding that existed between them, which was destined to last a lifetime.

Chapter 13

Ed was waiting at the Wheeler's Point boat ramp for Dave and Bill to arrive and in only moments they had the boat securely strapped back on the trailer, heading for Baudette with that rental winch fixed firmly in place on top of the boat. At the first empty road side park they stopped and packed all their treasure in large black plastic bags, filling the entire car's trunk. Three fifty pound bags of gold, which they weighed with their fish scale, were then placed under the seats in the boat, anticipating they'd each separately put those bags in a safety deposit box in Baudette, just to be on the safe side.

"That will serve as our rainy day measure in case we run into some untold problem on our trip back to the Twin Cities," Dave said.

Dave had taken out one nugget and a few gold flakes to have assayed at a local jewelry store in Baudette to be sure the gold was authentic, and even though he was certain it was, they were all anxious to find out the purity of their find. Once they reached Baudette, they returned the winch, paying the ten dollars they'd agreed to, and then they each rented a safety deposit box for their three fifty pound bags, breathing a little easier for the first time since finding this unbelievable fortune where little if any gold had ever been found before. A local jeweler next confirmed Dave's nugget that he said he found in Banff, as 24 Karat and 100 percent pure gold, which was of the same high quality Dave had found the previous year — and for the first time they were now absolutely certain their lives would never be the same. Once again they rented rooms at the Walleye Inn, and after showering, they set out to celebrate a bit at Rosalie's Restaurant. During dinner they talked about how this would inevitably change their lives and each of them already had some philanthropic idea they shared.

"I have no idea of just how much all this gold will be worth," Dave said, "but as the jeweler said it would be foolish for us to exchange this for today's fiat paper money, which may soon be worthless."

"Yah," Ed laughed. "I particularly liked the part where he said we may soon be papering our bathroom walls with today's hundred dollar bills."

"Well I liked the part where he said gold is selling between sixteen and seventeen hundred dollars an ounce, and if we do go into a depression gold might someday reach eight thousand dollars an ounce," Bill whispered so no one else could hear — grinning slyly as his eyes scanned the room to be sure no one was listening.

"At that price I guess we'll have to accurately weigh it before we split it into equal shares, and I agree, we'd be foolish to exchange it for money." Dave scowled. "I know that fifty pounds felt pretty damn heavy when I put it in my safety deposit box, and we've got a lot more to weigh in that trunk."

"If I calculated correctly, the value of what I put in that bank today would be somewhere near one million two hundred and eighty thousand dollars," Bill groaned, rolling both eyes as if in shock.

"And I bet we've got ten times that for each of us in the trunk," Dave added.

"No wonder the back bumper of the car is almost touching the ground." Ed chuckled as he looked out the window to be sure no one was bothering their car.

"Dave," Bill said, looking at him and asking, "What makes you think that we own all this treasure, I've heard these treasures can get pretty complex once you try to spend them."

Dave drew in a deep breath and slowly blew it out as he leaned back in his chair. "I knew this would come up sooner or later, and we might as well talk about it sooner than later, because it's bound to be on your mind if we don't decide on a single strategy we can all agree on." As he leaned forward he placed both elbows on the table and talked softly so he couldn't be overheard by anyone in the restaurant. "As I've told you before, the copper mining company I work for has a contract with the Government of Canada, which grants them the right to search out minerals in that area of Canada. You've seen my contract with the copper mining company, and since they are focused on copper like a laser, they have indicated in my agreement that if I find any valuable minerals, I can keep them as a benefit, since I'm not paid that much in the first place. Besides that, they know damn well there's very little if any gold or silver in this part of Canada, and the chance that I'd find any gold is next to none in their mind. My contract to search out copper in the Banff area doesn't have this same clause in it, and it doesn't take a genius to figure out why." Dave paused a moment to take a quick sip of beer before continuing.

"So in essence they've granted me sole rights to any gold I find in our magic pond area. And that's just exactly what has happened." With that Dave sat back and cleared his throat. "So, here is what we have to agree on," he continued once again leaning forward as if he was about to share still another big secret. "At this point and time, we cannot be certain that all this stuff we have found is gold, and we won't really know that until we have every ounce of this stuff analyzed by some licensed person who is qualified to do just that. And both the jeweler and I agree that it would be wise to not exchange gold for money for a couple reasons. One, gold is far more valuable than the U.S. dollar, which today is valued at about seventy six cents. And two, gold is very likely to gain substantially in value over the next few years. So here is my strategy, which I hope we can all agree on."

With that Dave paused and stared at the table in thought for a moment, rubbing at his beard before continuing.

"We need to hire a technically capable expert who can take this material, on an as needed basis, and analyze it for quality and provide accurate assaying that protects our interests, which we still have to decide. I've already agreed to split this evenly and yet I suggest we establish a sub chapter S non-profit foundation from which we can benefit others, and yet receive proper reimbursement for our services. The person or company we select to assay our material should also be able to take this raw material and melt it down into accurate weight modules that can be readily exchanged if and when needed. But for now, I suggest we sleep on what I've just suggested and discuss it later, as Dave stood up, ending the evening with much more to discuss.

The next morning, after breakfast, they drove to Bear Claws Reservation, and fortunately found him at home. After Dave introduced Bill and Ed, he went on to describe how they were checking the minerals out at the stream, when the pond suddenly disappeared.

Bear Claw's face turned ashen, as he mumbled, "*Nanabozho!* Only a spirit full of tricks could cause such a thing to happen."

"Yes, but then in only a little over a week, the stream returned," Dave continued.

Bear Claw looked confused, as if Dave was playing tricks on him and couldn't be trusted.

Dave could see this and he quickly added, "And we now think we know what happened." Pausing a moment Dave nervously adjusted his position in his chair so he was looking straight at Bear Claw who was still staring at him in disbelief. "And because we were so close to your reservation, we thought we'd drive here today and tell you what we believe happened before we returned to the Twin Cities."

Bear Claw nodded, clearly distrusting Dave for the first time.

"You see when the stream disappeared we found this giant hole in the ground with this huge meteorite type stone lying right in the center of the pond. But as we stood and stared at the huge hole in the ground we could still hear water running deep in the earth, and Bill, who is familiar with caves in the ground said it was an underground stream or an aquifer as he called it." Once again Dave nervously adjusted his position as he asked Bill to explain.

Still looking very confused by all this, Chief Bear Claw's stare focused on Bill without even uttering a word as his eyes became even more intense.

"Well, what was obvious to me was this huge meteor had fallen from the sky and cracked the earth crust. This allowed the underground stream that was flowing deep in the ground to push itself up to the surface and create this magic stream in which we were searching for copper minerals." Bill paused to give the Chief time to think a moment. "My thought is that since the Rocky Mountains to the west have had little rain or snow over the last year, and they were in a severe drought condition in that the water shed that feeds this underground river lacked water — it dried up enough to where it could no longer push water up to the surface. However, with all the rain we had last week in the mountains and here, the water pressure returned and forced the water back up to the surface, which allowed the stream to return on the very day we were going to leave."

With that Chief Bear Claw nodded, amazed that Bill had confirmed the same light in the sky that his father had described so many moons ago.

"What's so exciting about this, and why we came here to tell you, is we feel this aquifer runs deep in the ground under the Lake of the Woods below the granite shell of the earth, and from everything we can determine this same stream probably runs deep in the ground under your property, Bill said, watching Bear Claw's head nod several times, finally accepting what Bill was saying.

"We thought that if we could help you find this underground aquifer, we could dig a well and you could drink this pure spring water in place of the lake water you now drink." With that Dave quickly unfolded his map. "From our calculations we think this aquifer probably runs very close to the south side of Buffalo Bay. In fact we also think this same underground stream of pure water may also run all the way to Lake Superior, under Chief White Clouds Reservation."

With this they could see a sparkle of light in Bear Clouds eyes, as his wrinkled ashen face finally brightened into a smile.

"I have a tribe member who uses tree branches to find such things and I will have him search for this magic stream you call an aquifer," The Chief finally responded.

Bill was quick to point out the location on the map where he thought they might find the underground stream, while Dave told him how he planned to stop by White Clouds Reservation and tell him where he might also search for this same magic water.

Arriving in Duluth later that afternoon, they found the streets filled with protesters carrying signs saying that the one percent of wealthy international corporate families controlled almost all of the money in America. The police were trying to disperse the crowds with tear gas and it took a good hour to find their way around the crowded streets to get to the North Shore Drive, which would take them to White Cloud's Reservation. Ed had grabbed a pamphlet from one of the protesters and was busily reading it as Dave turned and looked at Ed and Bill.

"I hate to suggest we spend another night at a motel and risk another night on the road with all this treasure," he added, "but it would be much later than I'd like to arrive at White Cloud's Reservation if we don't stop and stay somewhere tonight."

"Well let's at least drive out of Duluth with all these protesters here, and stop at a motel on the North Shore," Bill suggested. "And to be on the safe side maybe I could sleep in the car to protect our loot."

"Hell, I'd fit much better in the back seat than you would, and I've been wanting to find a reason to use this gun I bought anyway," Ed scoffed, settling any further discussion as to who'd sleep in the car.

At dinner that night they began to share their thoughts for the first time as to what they might do with all their new found wealth.

Dave explained, "I have a desire to help these poor Indians who suffer from arsenic poisoning and lung cancer. They need a clinic and a specialist right on the reservation to treat them and maybe assist in getting some of the younger Chippewa's lung transplants. I don't intend to tell White Cloud this just yet, but I just may surprise him someday."

Bill had been thinking of going on to medical school, and yet he had a lot of concern with the recent changes that had taken place in medicine — from a once respected profession to a profit seeking Insurance controlled business. "I just don't believe that profiting from the sick and disabled is the right way to go. I've been doing a lot of reading on this lately and I'm still a strong proponent of the Hippocratic Oath."

Ed was last to describe his interest. "You know, I'd always thought I'd end up in the banking business, yet I'm surely not one who believes in these *Too Big to Fail Banks*. In fact, these International Investment Bankers are the ones who are causing what we just witnessed in Duluth, and I believe it's going to get much worse before it gets better. And if I could, I'd damned well like to do something about that."

The next morning they arrived at Chief White Clouds Reservation and the Chief was very pleased to see Dave and meet his two friends. Dave was anxious to hear how things were going for him and his tribes, and he surprised Dave by telling him that most of his Arsenic poisoned patients were getting much better. It wasn't the same for those that had developed lung cancer from the Taconite tailings, but even they were at least holding their own much better and not dying as fast as they were when Dave first found out about their dreadful problem. Dave had noticed the same water cans that Bear Claw had on his reservation and immediately suspected something.

"May I ask where you got those water cans?" Dave asked, feeling he knew White Cloud well enough to ask.

"Yes, I'm surprised you noticed. We've been concerned about our drinking water lately and so we've had our ill patients drink some spring water we've brought in. In fact, Bear Claw brought this to us in these milk cans, telling us it had healing capability, so we've been trying it, and he just may be right."

With that, Dave spread his map out on the table, telling White Cloud about the stream they were studying and how it suddenly disappeared. Then after asking White Cloud for a ruler he placed one end on the glacier area north of Banff and the center of the ruler where they were checking for minerals in the magic stream that disappeared. Then by running his finger along the ruler he showed White Cloud how it went across his reservation almost exactly where they were standing.

We think this Aquifer that Bear Claw gets his healing water from runs from that glacier near Banff under the crust of the earth all the way to Lake Superior where it empties right about here. If you'll notice, the Rainy River follows this same direction. So we think you could drill for a well about here, and possibly tap into this same aquifer, obtaining pure spring fed water for your tribe from these glaciers in northern Alberta. If you'd like, I'd be willing to come back here someday and perhaps help you accomplish this, which would be better than drinking the lake water. Another thing I'd like to do is have one of your tribe members train to become a physician so you could have your own clinic and no longer have to go all the way to the St. Joe's or St Luke's Hospitals in Duluth all the time.

White Cloud nodded approvingly, openly holding back his emotions.

After they left the White Cloud Reservation Ed reminded them of how his welts from the fly bites disappeared after his disastrous swim in the pond.

"You remember those bites on my neck were pretty severe, and suddenly they were gone. Do you think there could be something to this magic water these Indians are carting all the way to their reservations?

"Hell, we probably should have asked for a sample of that water so we could get it analyzed as well as the gold," Dave said. "But I can get that on my next trip up here. Who knows, maybe we have another Lourdes of France, right in our own backyard."

As they drove back to the Twin Cities Ed spent much of the trip silently studying the Duluth pamphlet that was handed to him by one of the protesters.

"I think it might help if we each read this Duluth handout I picked up. I find it very interesting and it just might help us make some decisions regarding our future," Ed said, handing it to Dave. "It's called *Our Political Stress Syndrome*."

Chapter 14

OUR POLITICAL STRESS SYNDROME (PSS)
By
We the People

The United States and the rest of the world currently find themselves in a sustainability crisis that will destroy the ecological balance for human life on earth if we do not take steps to correct these problems we are all so stressed out about. These problems first reared there ugly head in the United States when our politicians ignored our Democracy and created a privately owned Federal Reserve Bank in nineteen thirteen; ignored the oil commodities problems and our country's natural resource rights as far back as the nineteen thirties; and then deregulated and decentralized our health care system in nineteen forty-five. And now our politicians are completely ignoring our global environment through their intentional disregard for our air quality and climate; the misuse of our environmental energy, water and the food chain; and their intentionally deregulating and decentralizing of our healthcare, transportation, education and retirement systems. What's even worse is with today's exponentially growing population of seven billion human beings we are becoming seriously out of balance with the finite number of global resources this planet can ever provide. Our global population is projected to reach 13 billion by 2075, and 26 billion in 2145, which is well beyond this earth's capability to support. Long range projections suggest that if population growth continues at this current rate there will be one human being for every square meter of earth's land surface by 3050, which of course will never occur since humanity will have ceased well before that unless we find another planet to over-populate.

*And yet **We the People** have yet to demand an adequate Master Plan from our totally dysfunctional leaders who seek to create a New World Order (NWO), which will never succeed in their reckless attempt to rule the World. Hasn't every major empire previously tried to do this and always failed?*

If you've studied history you already know that Democracies usually last no more than two hundred and fifty years because those that become very wealthy eventually seek to control, protect and expand their wealth at the cost of others. They accomplish this through deregulation and decentralization, which eventually forces the people into a two level system; one for the deregulated and tax free rich and one for the very regulated and over taxed middle class who actually work to provide the basic human services needed for our survival.

OUR FINANCIAL CRISES

*Today, this country's Congress, Senate, and Federal Reserve are owned and controlled by a very tightly knit group of International Investment Bankers including Goldman Sachs, The Rothschild Group, Morgan Stanley, JP Morgan Chase, Citigroup, Bank of America, Wells Fargo, and the Union Bank of Switzerland (UBS) where they all meet annually. Together, they financially control a majority of the world's International Corporations as well as all their **Too Big to Fail** (TBTF) investment banks. This type of financial control was first* *attempted in 1934, when many of these very same bankers and corporations attempted to unseat President Roosevelt in a plot that was publicly exposed by retired Marine Corps Major General Smedley Butler when he spoke before the McCormack-Dickstein Congressional Committee. In his testimony, Butler told this committee on July 17, 1932, that he was approached by several wealthy businessmen who had asked him to help overthrow our Democracy in a military coup. In the Congressional Committee's report Butler's allegations were later validated, but no prosecutions or further investigations ever followed, which is usually what happens when it involves this upper crust. In retrospect, the devastation of the Great Depression had caused many of these very rich families to question the foundation of our Democracy, considering Fascism, Socialism, or even Communism as an alternative that would give them greater control over their wealth. Yet even today, many of these same wealthy international investment bankers are still directly involved in today's fiscal insolvency through their privately owned Federal Reserve. They have also achieved substantial control over much of this nation's gold since we went off our gold standard, and they continue to aggressively seek total control over the World Market, the International Industrial Complex, and our Nation's Armed Services. Do you remember when America once set an example for other nations to follow, without buying off and suppressing other nations with our military force? Do you remember how after World War II, this nation openly vowed to never go to war unless we were attacked — yet these international business leaders have somehow blamelessly maneuvered the U.S. into some seventeen conflicts with Vietnam, Cambodia, Laos, Philippines, Somalia, Haiti, Croatia, Bosnia, Chechnya, Albania, Kosovo, Serbia, Sudan, Iraq, Afghanistan, East Timor, and Libya since World War II. Haven't we even noticed how our once peace loving nation has become the most warring nation on earth? Don't we remember how this same subversive culture also influenced a group of neoconservatives to start today's unjust and never ending war with Afghanistan and then Iraq — resulting in today's eternal religious conflicts that we can no longer become free of? And now, even after all this, this same subversive culture is still promoting several more provocations to send our weakened U.S. Military into another perpetual religious conflict with Iran, or perhaps North Korea or one of several other religious conflicts currently raging in the Middle East. Isn't it time for us to just pause a moment and try to recognize what's really going on under the control of this informal enemy within? Or should we just stand idly by in our constant state of fear and stress while these aggressive entrepreneurs kill thousands and annihilate so many other country's industrial and social structures for years to come — just so they can control or market these weaker nation's natural resources? In fact, more recently they've successfully kept most Americans so focused on our dysfunctional two party system and our costly and meaningless elections that we can no longer recognize the covert dominance of this International Oligarchy that clearly intends to level our once admired Republic to that of other nations. And haven't you noticed how those that try to stop their money making schemes and wars are quickly labeled isolationists or socialists? Yet, We the People continue to be taxed for our armed services that unconsciously conduct their dirty work without our nation ever being attacked. Why? Because wars produced huge sums of money for this Oligarchic group of powerful international investment bankers.*

After Bill and Dave both read the Duluth handout they sat contemplating the dangers ahead in misusing the potential wealth that had been miraculously handed to them as a result of their unbelievable summer adventure.

"And if we have fifteen hundred pounds of gold in our trunk, we're going to be very rich," Bill said, pursing his lips and thoughtfully gazing off into space. "My guess is we have close to forty-two million at today's gold price if we include what we put in the safety deposit vault the other day. I don't even want to try and calculate what we could be worth if what that jeweler said about future gold prices turns out to be right."

"And I can't stop thinking of what we might find if we ever get another chance to go down into that magic hole again, or if we by some miraculous chance of fate do find where that underground aquifer empties into Lake Superior," Dave added.

"So we've got some serious decisions to make," Ed interrupted. "Don't we? — And that means we not only have to decide what we individually want to do, but if it might be advantageous for us to work together as Dave suggested."

"I have a feeling our worries are just beginning," Bill scowled. "If the wealthy really do worry more about protecting their treasure, than being ethical and perhaps helping humankind, we could become just as irresponsible as this *Political Stress Syndrome* article suggests."

"So what are we going to do about it?" Dave asked.

"I think we have to make our decisions in stages," Ed suggested. "First we have to shore up and secure this potential treasure, and then decide our individual needs before we can expect to set any future goals — be they either mercenary or philanthropic. The number one question is do we trade gold for cash and invest it after we pay tax, or do we store it in a safe place where it might gain in value over time — not knowing its true value for sure until it goes under the scrutiny of some qualified assessor who can melt it down into standard gold bars. And if we aren't going to trade it for cash, we need to think of where we'll store it as individuals or as perhaps a nonprofit foundation, where we'd take adequate salaries and donate the vast majority to causes that merit some philanthropic purpose toward mankind as a whole."

"I think we should go the foundation route," Dave was quick to reply. "I think we should continue to find more of this stuff and help White Cloud find his magic stream and take care of those sick Indians. This whole damn thing has had so much *Divine* intervention in it that I feel something or someone is guiding us. If you think about it, you have to agree — don't you?"

"I can't disagree with you, but we also don't want to go down that road and then later disagree," Bill added.

"Hell, if we keep the treasure in a vault, we can always split it up later if we wish. But going the Foundation route with salaries will require some long range commitment by all of us," Ed grimaced, still very much undecided.

"Ed, you said you wanted to be in banking," Dave cut in, "and if the three of us all became the Board of Directors and you the Executive Director of the Foundation, would you be satisfied with that?"

"Perhaps," Ed replied, still obviously needing more time to think about that.

"I like the idea of looking for more gold, and if Dave builds that well for Bear Claw, we could probably search the magic pond every time we filled Bear Claws water tower," Bill chuckled, leaning towards Dave's foundation concept. "I'd also like to see us build a foundation office on the North Shore Drive, near where we just might find this magic stream dumps into Lake Superior. That would also be close enough to White Cloud's Reservation so we could help him find that magic aquifer and perhaps build that clinic for his tribe."

"Brilliant," Dave shouted. "You've just outlined our future!" he grinned as Bill pulled the car to a stop on the shoulder.

"Let's vote right now," Bill suggested, "before we get anymore suggestions."

"Wait a minute," Ed shouted, "that's no way to do business."

"The hell it ain't!" Dave bellowed, turning to stare Ed down in the back seat. "I think we've already got a two to one vote unless you want to take your share and skip town."

"I just may do that, but at least let me think about it overnight," Ed growled, knowing that if he was to continue as a member of the team, he'd have to make a decision soon.

"Alright," Bill replied, as he put the car back in gear and pulled back on the highway. "Dave, are we in agreement on this?"

"Of course we are," Dave shouted, "let's cash in enough of your treasure and mine to build that foundation on Lake Superior, and we'll get started digging those wells and building that damn clinic of yours."

"Wait a minute," Ed shouted. "You can't just vote me out like that." Then after a long pause he added. "Alright damn it, so you've just hired the new Executive Director of *The Kitchimanadoo Foundation*."

With that both Bill and Dave doubled up laughing, "Where in the hell did you get that name, Dave asked still laughing as he talked.

"Well isn't that the name of the Great Spirit that Bear Claw told us leads his tribes. And Isn't that the same damned Spirit that sure as hell has been the *Devine* power behind all we've gone through this summer — ever since Bill first complained about his boat being too heavy to get us to Split Rock?"

The next morning, Ed set out to incorporate a nonprofit corporation for tax purposes and find a corporate attorney that would provide all the necessary legal guidance to incorporate a *Sub-Chapter S* corporation. Later that same day he opened the foundation's bank account at one of the largest banks in the Twin Cities, and since confidentiality was of the highest priority, he made both the assayer and attorney agree to this in their contracts.

Later, the three of them all sat down with the new attorney to discuss what would be required of them by their new Articles of Incorporation and By-Laws. The attorney also advised them that a safe deposit box was a matter of public record, and that a bank can be presented with a court order, which would obligate them by law to release all account information including the safe deposit box number as well as the branch where it was located.

"Within a matter of hours, access to your box could be frozen and in the event of a financial crisis or national emergency, the government could declare a "bank holiday" to prevent the collapse of the banking system," the attorney said.

Since this actually had happened in 1929, Ed was very concerned that if this were to occur in the near future, they'd be unable to access their safe deposit box. So that suggested he immediately acquire a large enough vault to hold their treasure even though he had no immediate place to store such a vault. However, public storage offered a temporary solution so he had the vault delivered to a public storage facility, until they could decide on the actual location they'd build their Foundation on.

After this meeting with their attorney they hurriedly traveled back to Baudette, where each emptied their safe deposit boxes before returning right back to the Twin Cities. Late that same afternoon, they carried all their unprocessed gold from their trunk into their apartment where they placed their treasure temporarily in the bath tub and locked the bathroom door. Next they had their assayer process the one hundred and fifty pounds of unprocessed gold they'd just picked up in Baudette, so they'd soon have the necessary assets to get things started.

Dave next scheduled separate meetings with Bear Claw and White Cloud to discuss their philanthropic plans in greater detail.

"If we can find that magic aquifer on your reservation," Dave explained to Bear Claw, "we'd be willing to build, and operate a water tower and the necessary pumps to provide you fresh clean spring water every day. We'd also be willing to pay for the necessary maintenance, and we'd like to hire a member of your tribe to do just that. But first we have to see if that aquifer actually runs under Lake of the Woods like we think it does."

"As I told you, one of our tribe members is very good at Water Witching," Bear Claw said. "He uses a Y shaped branch from a willow tree and grasps this branch with his palms down, like this," Bear Claw explained as he demonstrated by holding his hands as the tribe member did. "Then he walks very slowly over the places he's searching to find water — and once he's over ground water the twig dips or twitches and I can tell you he very seldom fails. In fact many people have hired him to find water," Chief Bear Claw nodded as he spoke, obviously suggesting Dave use him to help find the magic stream that he believed was running right under Bear Claw's reservation. "He can even tell which direction the stream flows." Bear Claw added, as his wife served the sandwiches she'd previously prepared for their visit.

During lunch, Dave also told Bear Claw of his plans to build *The Kitchimanadoo Foundation* on Lake Superior and once again the Chief seemed pleased. "We're also going to provide the material and equipment to help White Cloud build a clinic and train a doctor," Dave added. Next he took out his map and showed the Chief how the underground aquifer could flow all the way to Lake Superior, also crossing right under White Cloud's property. "If your tribe member is successful in locating this stream for you, perhaps he could help us find the same stream we think runs under White Cloud's reservation," Dave explained as Bear Claw nodded in agreement. "What we'd like to do, if he finds this magic stream, is have our foundation donate all the necessary equipment and material so you both can build the necessary water towers that could supply your villages."

Needless to say, they were all in total agreement before they left for Grand Marais later that same day, where Ed would next began his search for lake shore property to build their Foundation.

Chapter 15

In 1889, more than a century ago, the federal government made a settlement with the <u>Chippewa</u> nation of Minnesota regarding a land and timber treaty – but this settlement was never honored, and as a result, the U.S. still owed millions of dollars to the <u>Chippewa</u> tribe. More recently, the Congress ended debating a possible $28 million payment to more than 40,000 Chippewa members that could each receive $300 with some $16 million going to the <u>Chippewa</u> government. However, payment still remained highly unlikely in that the current Congress will probably never pay a lump sum of $28 million in today's turbulent times. In fact today's dysfunctional Congress is well aware that the <u>Chippewa</u> nation has already been beaten down by violence, illness and disease, and many members have always hoped the Indians would just go away, or just accept their sub-human status in society. In fact, this is where the term "Indian giver" was finally born in the twentieth century because of the Congresses' chronic failure to comply with these witnessed contracts. And this is why the Minnesota Chippewa Tribe continues to bring their allegations and complaints to the Indian Claims Commission. As a result, these claims eventually formed the basis for the federal government's 1999 agreement to pay the Chippewa, but now, the government still hasn't honored its decision. So the more recent court finding was the direct result of the federal government's miss-management of the <u>1889 Nelson Allotment Act</u>, under which some reservation land was ceded to the United States, with the *land value to go into a trust fund for the Chippewa. But of course that never happened, and so the federal court found in 1999 that this deal shortchanged the Chippewa tribes, and as a result they have once again actually awarded a $28 million-dollar settlement. The land settlement included the tip of Minnesota's Arrowhead country, known as the Grand Portage Band, which included White Cloud's Tribe — however, many individual Chippewa still do not find much comfort in what they see as pathetically deficient compensation for what their ancestors lost. Many believe the District Court is just trying to make legitimate the theft of Indian land — while no amount of money or land could ever repay any Native American community for all the bigotry and exploitation they've endured.*

As previously indicated, Taconite is a flint-type rock containing low-grade iron ore; and huge reserves of taconite with iron concentrations of 30-50% were discovered in Minnesota in 1870. However, at that time they decided not to mine this ore because it was of little value since extracting the iron was extremely difficult and far too costly. Then in 1940, scientists developed a cost-effective method of removing the iron from taconite by "pelletizing" the ore. As a result, the Reserve Mining Company built, in the late 1950s, a taconite processing plant at Silver Bay, Minnesota — where they eventually processed up to 10 million tons of pellets a year, while disposing of the powdered remains — the tailings — into Lake Superior. Until 1980, the Reserve Mining Company had been permitted to dump up to 67,000 tons of tailings a day directly into the lake, ruining the once-pristine waters of Lake Superior. In fact, fish were dying and people were very upset by the pollution it was causing. In 1969, the Sierra Club, with several other groups, filed a suit to force the Minnesota Pollution Control Agency to apply standards set forth in the Water Quality Act of 1965. The resulting suit lasted through

April 1982, pitting governments and citizen organizations against steel companies, the Iron Range communities, and the United Steelworkers union. Eventually this dispute became so heated that claims were made that "asbestos-like" fibers released from the tailings had reached western Lake Superior and filtered into the municipal water systems of Duluth and surrounding communities. The ensuing cancer scare and a potential federal trial garnered national attention as plaintiffs and defendants considered the effects of the pollution, the socioeconomic consequences of alternative waste sites, and the possibility of closing an industry on which an entire region depended. In 1972, the United States government had previously sued the Reserve Mining Company, under the Rivers and Harbors Act of 1899, for disposing of harmful materials into Lake Superior. Because of all this negative public relations, the mining company eventually was forced to find another location to dump their tailings just west of Silver Bay, in a land locked area about five miles from Lake Superior, where they could more confidently dispose of the potentially carcinogenic taconite tailings. However, it was impossible for the company to remove the already dispersed taconite tailings from the lake.

Later, the Minnesota Pollution Control Agency (MPCA) also claimed the plant exceeded permitted levels for the tailing dust, which came from moving and stockpiling the taconite pellets in this new area. As a result the company was ordered to pay $240,000 in fines for violating air quality standards — forcing the company to began using more water and chemical dust suppressants to keep the dust down. In 1985, The Reserve Mining Company did obtain permission to pump filtered overflow water from the tailings pond back into Lake Superior, but with all the controversy the mining operation was eventually forced to close in 1986. Then in 1999, the facility *reopened on a smaller scale as Northshore Mining, which still produces taconite pellets; however, many questions still remain about the health and ecological effects of taconite tailings. Northshore Mining is currently looking at the possibility of selling their coarse tailings as aggregate to construct roads and combat slippery winter driving, or using the tailings in a concrete mix if deemed safe for such commercial use.*

Ed had rented a car and a motel where they could all stay at Grand Marais on the coast of Lake Superior, while Bill and Dave drove some seventeen miles up the Gunflint Trail to meet with Chief White Cloud at his home on Northern Light Lake. The Gunflint trail was a sixty miles long dirt road, going all the way to the northern border of the Arrowhead Country and ending at Gunflint Lake, where Dave had often spent his summers portaging from lake to lake while searching for copper in some of the most beautiful and pristine lake and forest country in the world.

White Cloud was very supportive to their *Kitchimanadoo Foundation* as well as all the benefits he'd derive from Dave's desire to help his tribe fight off the many healthcare problems they'd encountered over the years. Tapping into the magic aquifer was something he was particularly excited about, in that it would mean a new source of fresh spring water to replace the lake water they'd been using for far too long. As Dave described in detail how he intended to find the aquifer by using electronic signals, he explained how he planned to send floats that emitted electronic signals down the aquifer from the magic pond — which really excited Bill because this was the first time he'd heard about it and it was also a perfect solution to find where the aquifer emptied into Lake Superior.

If we can find that location, there just may be more gold waiting for us, and that's where we should acquire land for our foundation, Bill thought. *And if that location were near Grand Marais, we'd be near an airport, which would make it easy to travel to the twin cities from this beautiful but remote location.*

"You're welcome to build your foundation right next to that clinic on our reservation," Chief White Cloud suggested as Bill and Dave prepared to leave.

"You're very kind to offer that," Dave replied. "And we'll keep that in mind if we can't find an adequate location on the shoreline of Lake Superior."

Ed had accumulated all kinds of information about land acquisition in the Arrowhead Country, and as they sat down to eat that evening he explained — "Apparently the properties available for purchase change hands quickly, and most of the owners are not financially able to enter into any long term decision with the State — so I suspect there may be some private land available around Grand Marais if that's where we decide to locate."

"Do we need to get a prospector's permit like the companies that I currently do prospecting for?" Dave asked.

"Perhaps, and the Bureau of Land Management issues those permits. In fact, all prospecting has to abide by the protection specified in this environmental impact statement they gave me," Ed said, waving the document up in the air as he continued. "It says here that this document was developed by a whole slew of partners including The Trust for Public Land; The Conservation Fund; The Nature Conservancy; The Friends of the Boundary Waters; The Minnesota Historical Society; The Minnesota Department of Natural Resources; The Leech Lake Area Watershed Foundation; The Izaak Walton

League; as well as a very large list of local communities and action groups."

"Wow!" Dave replied with a discouraged grunt. "My contract lists me as a prospector in this area and allows me to take and keep samples, but it draws the line on mining."

"Dave, I think we should have our attorney check out your contract, but thank God we at least have it," Bill interrupted. "You know, that document could eventually prove very valuable to us, and it may also prove important you try to keep that agreement in place in the years ahead, particularly if we intend to do more prospecting along the Lake Superior shoreline. And yes, I suppose we should also investigate what's involved in obtaining a permit to mine gold from Lake Superior, just in case we happen to really strike it rich," Bill added, looking at Ed.

"I know The Bureau of Land Management doesn't authorize mining permits — just prospecting." Ed said. "It's some federal agency that issues all drilling permits, even though all mining proposals go through a separate environmental review by the Bureau of Land Management." With that Ed paused to once again study the document. "There is also a long environmental impact statement on the effects of prospecting for copper, nickel, platinum and related minerals in the Superior National Forest, and after reading it I'd suggest that in the future we only speak of related minerals instead of gold, because no one even thinks there's gold in them there hills." Ed smirked as he spoke. "And I can just see us starting a 49'rs gold rush all over again, if we ever let that little secret out of the bag."

"You're right about that," Dave agreed. "So what you're saying is we really need to keep this thing close to the vest from here on out. — Don't we? Particularly with our attorney and that assayer we hired — is that agreed?" Dave asked, looking at both Bill and Ed.

As Bill and Ed simultaneously nodded they both replied, "Absolutely," fully appreciating for the first time the importance of entering into such a confidential pact between them.

Back in the Twin Cities, Dave spent much of his time studying world tracking solutions, looking at a variety of real time GPS systems that were revolutionizing current tracking technology. He was particularly interested in an ultra small size rugged designed splash resistant unit that included an internal Pelican battery pack that provided up to 6 months of tracking on one battery charge. Best of all, he found there was no software to install. All you had to do was call the number indicated and you'd be provided with secure online access to watch your unit in real-time as it traveled down the aquifer. And better yet, there was only a $70.00 activation fee with unlimited tracking for just $50.00 a month.

He also found a new Electro-Seismic technology used to find groundwater, by setting off a black powder charge that sent a sound pressure wave 1500 feet deep from four one meter long electrodes that were strategically placed in the ground that were hooked up to a special computer. The computer recorded data from each electrode at various selected sites on ones property. The data would then be processed with a detailed report telling where to drill, how deep to drill and even what water yield could be expected at each site, like 25 gallons per minute.

This sounds a hell of a lot better than using witches and dowsers with forked sticks or metal rods. With this unit we'd be able to search Bear Claw's Reservation and even estimate the gallons per minute, Dave thought.

Since the most important task was to locate the magic stream, Dave and Bill set out with their new equipment to spend time at Bear Claws Reservation, while Ed began the planning for the construction of their Foundation and their new Clinic at White Clouds Reservation even though they hadn't yet finalized any locations. Dave had already talked to several companies that were capable of building water towers and he had a good idea of what it would involve if they located the aquifer.

"Mior, has already found what he believes is a powerful underground stream of water running under the south side of Buffalo Bay," Bear Claw said anxious to let Dave know that what he'd told Dave earlier was accurate. "He thinks it runs right under the ground where we hold our meetings."

"Is Mior the Indian that uses witching sticks? Dave asked.

"Yes, it took him only a short time to find what he's certain is a very fast running underground stream," Bear Claw grinned as he explained that Mior's name meant *Rippling Brook.*

"I have some equipment I've brought with me that can confirm his find and even tell how many gallons of water flow through the ground per minute, and I'll need his help to accomplish that if he's available," Dave explained, knowing that it would not be good to question Mior's find.

This is remarkable, Bill thought, *we already have a potential location to drill and we've just arrived.*

"Do you know anyone who can drill a well?" Bill asked the Chief.

"Mior does, and I'm sure he can get him to help," Bear Claw nodded as he spoke.

By early afternoon, Dave and Mior had already confirmed Mior's find and the report indicated that the water was approximately fifty feet below the surface and the gallons per minute were far in excess of 25, which meant that this could well be the magic stream.

"I can't believe things are going this easy," Bill whispered to Dave.

"I know, and once we get a drill down there and open up things we can send this GPS system on its way while you go to the magic stream on the other side of the lake and confirm that we have the right location."

"God this is really getting exciting," Bill chuckled.

"I bet that float will pop right out of the ground into the magic pond," Dave chuckled as he thought about it. "But I haven't even thought about how we can send it on its way to Lake Superior unless this one decides to go all the way."

"Well let's get this part of the plan done first and then we can figure that out later," Bill replied.

It took several days of drilling to open the right size hole in the ground which would then have to be capped properly while Dave confirmed the final arrangements to build the water tower and then decide how to send his GPS system on its first trip. Bill had once again brought his boat with them, and both he and Dave decided to have Mior send the GPS float on its way, while they monitored its route in real time and then waited for it to pop to the surface at the magic pond. As they anxiously scanned the floats path, it soon became obvious that they had absolutely found the right aquifer, and just as planned the float suddenly popped to the surface of the magic pond. Using Bill's fish net they quickly recovered the GPS float and returned to tell Chief Bear Claw that he definitely now had the magic stream's water available for his Tribe on his own reservation. That evening the Chief called all his Tribes together to share the news and honor both Bill and Dave.

"The Great Kitchimanadoo has blessed us with the magic water we were given so many moons ago." Chief Bear Claw spoke forcefully as he stood tall in his full head dress near a huge bonfire where they were celebrating the occasion.

"The Great Kitchimanadoo has also blessed us with these two men who have brought us this great gift that we shall always treasure and honor in their behalf." With that the Chief paused to grasp both Bill and Dave's hands. "And they have also honored the *Ojibwe* on Chief White Cloud's Reservation in the Superior National Forest, where they have been besieged with sickness. These men next plan to build a clinic and perhaps find this same Great Kitchimanadoo's water for them."

With that Chief Bear Claw pulled a knife from his belt and cut his thumb, doing the same with both Dave and Bill as they stood dumbfounded, not knowing what to do.

"We are all privileged to accept you as *Blood Brothers,* who will always be welcome here," he spoke respectfully, pressing his thumb against first Dave's bleeding thumb and then Bill's, blending their blood with his.

At that the tribe erupted as their drums sent out a message that could be heard for miles, while the celebration continued late into the night.

Chapter 16

As Bill and Dave studied the magic pond they could see it was going to be very difficult to send the GPS float on to the Arrowhead country against the rushing water that was surging up from under the ground.

"What if we bought six ten foot lengths of plastic pipe and glued them all together and then lowered one end of it down into the aquifer," Bill suggested. "That way we could have Mior drop the GPS float down the pipe into the current that flows toward Lake Superior and you could monitor its route in real time to see if it reaches White Cloud's Reservation — and I could monitor the lake's shoreline in my boat. Hopefully we could trace it to the exact spot where it finally pops up in Lake Superior. The instructions say that the signal can be monitored up to fifty miles, so I should certainly have time enough to motor to the exact spot the GPS enters the lake."

"That just might work," Dave agreed, "and it really doesn't matter if we don't find the float as long as we can accurately record its path," But as Dave reflected on that for a minute he thought better of what he'd just said. "But we should certainly try to find the float, if we can."

"I'm sure we will, haven't we been right about everything else we've guessed at so far?" Bill said, laughing and hoping they'd figured things out correctly one more time.

The next day Mior helped load six ten foot plastic pipes into Bill's boat, along with a good supply of pipe sealer before they set out to test Bill's pipe theory, still not sure that things would work out as he'd suggested.

After finding several spots in the aquifer where a few cork like test floats disappeared, they all agreed on a day and time that Mior would release the GPS float, while being in contact by cell phone on that day while everyone was on the same page in accomplishing their plan.

"I think this crazy idea just may work," Dave said with a tinge of excitement as they headed back to the reservation. "Wouldn't it be great if it all works out just as we planned?" he scoffed.

"You know it's for sure there's been some type of *Divine* intervention leading us toward this whole damned thing," Bill replied. "And if this is what we really should be doing, maybe we just might be able to someday turn a few things around in this crazy world we all try to exist in."

Before they left, the next day, Dave made all the necessary arrangements with the contractor to build Bear Claw's water tower, which would take at least a couple more months.

As Bill and Dave got into the car, Bear Claw thanked them several times, saying, "We'll see to it that Mior gets to the pond in time to send the GPS on its way, and I'll let you know if we have any problems finishing the water tower."

One week later, Dave arrived at White Cloud's Reservation, ready to monitor the GPS float, and Bill was standing near his boat ready and waiting for the first signals to show up on his monitor.

"Alright Mior, were ready at this end," Dave finally said, and in only moments Mior replied, "It's on its way."

Bill had estimated the float would have to travel well over two hundred miles to reach White Cloud's Reservation, and they had estimated the speed of the stream to be approximately twenty to twenty five miles an hour — so it could take at least eight hours before they might even expect to receive the first signal, if it didn't get stuck somewhere along the way.

After nine hours, Dave was getting discouraged, advising Bill that there was still no sign of anything on his monitor, when suddenly a small red dot appeared on the edge of his CRT screen.

"Oh my God," he shrieked, "We were right," he yelled at the top of his voice. "It's about fifty miles away and heading right at us," he shouted over his cell phone. "You should be able to see it on your monitor in the next hour, so you better get ready," Dave cried out joyfully, as he nervously described its steady movement on the monitor to Bill.

Bill could feel Dave's excitement as he hurried to get his boat ready. The westerly breezes were fairly strong and it took him much longer than he'd planned to pull away from the shore against some rather sizeable waves, and for a second he wished he'd asked White Cloud for one of his tribe members to help, since only one man in the boat could prove dangerous on Lake Superior, particularly if the unpredictable weather decided to act up. Yet they really wanted to keep the aquifer location secret and that wouldn't have been playing things close to the vest as they agreed, so he thought better of that once he was out where the large rolling waves were far less intimidating. Glancing at his monitor he still saw nothing.

Damn it, what if nothing showed up on his monitor, He thought to himself, and then suddenly he saw the first signal, about thirty miles northwest of White Clouds home. Unbelievably the signal was heading directly for White Cloud's property.

We were right all along, Bill whispered to himself, estimating that he might have to move as much as ten miles to the northeast to find the location where the GPS float would finally reach the mouth of the aquifer in Lake Superior. After motoring slowly in that direction he suddenly notice the signal take an abrupt turn to the south, just a mile or two from White Clouds home.

Dave confirmed the change in direction, yelling out loudly, "Bill, the aquifer has changed direction and it's now heading directly south."

"I read you loud and clear," Bill yelled back, as the breeze picked up and white caps began to appear on the top of some of the larger waves, which had not been much of a problem so far.

Hurriedly Bill turned the boat around and began moving to a location where he estimated the GPS was now heading. As he watched the little red signal move closer and closer to the shoreline, he realized what a remarkable accomplishment this whole thing was and he thanked the powers above that were obviously guiding them from the moment they first began this long mind-boggling journey. Then suddenly a huge wave pushed the boat up and down like a cork, sending a chill of urgency down Bill's spine as an ice cold spray of lake water washed across his face.

"That damn float better get here soon or I could be in real trouble," Bill yelled over his cell phone. "Dave, these damn waves are getting rather serious all of a sudden."

With that Dave jumped in White Cloud's car and sped down the dirt covered Gun Flint road, hoping to get to the lake in time to help Bill land by the boat ramp.

"Damn it, don't take any chances," Dave yelled over his phone as he treacherously raced the seventeen miles toward the lake and then still had to go several more miles northeast of Grand Marais. "In fact, once you see the float, just go back to your boat ramp and forget that damn float," he shouted, skidding wildly around each curve on the remote Gunflint Trail.

Then just as Bill was about to give up and head for shore, he saw the red and white float sliding down the back of a huge wave that was about to crash wildly against the granite rock shoreline.

"If I can just get a little closer I think I can net it with my fish net," he yelled, just as Dave shouted back, "Don't even think of that — just mark the location and get the hell out of there — we can always look for that GPS later, when things calm down."

Finally Dave wildly skidded onto Shoreline Drive, and in only a few miles he spotted Bill's Car parked by the boat ramp, where he screeched to a halt — running quickly down the ramp he scanned the brutally wild surface of the lake, looking for any sign of Bill and his boat, but there was none. Nervously he paced back and forth, once again trying to reach Bill on the phone, but there was no response. Then after about ten more minutes Dave finally spotted something cresting on what was a massive wave about fifty yards from shore, just as another gigantic wave crashed ashore, soaking Dave with a ton of ice cold lake water. The powerful surge knocked Dave off his feet, pushing him a good fifteen feet up the boat ramp. Awkwardly he slipped several times before finally standing up and rushing to Bill's car, where he swiftly searched out Bill's reserve set of keys and hurriedly backed the trailer into the water, where the waves were surging well above the car's wheels. As Bill's boat cautiously approached the ramp, he wildly aimed the boat at the submerged trailer, just before an even larger wave violently heaved the boat right over the trailer. No sooner than Dave saw the boat over the trailer he floored the accelerator, driving up the ramp and praying that the boat would somehow be pulled out of the water on top of the trailer. As luck would have it, the tide simultaneously sucked itself back toward the lake and the boat loudly slammed down right on top of the trailer. Looking in the rear view mirror, Dave thankfully watched the boat lurch out of the water, and move safely up the boat ramp with Bill grinning from ear to ear.

"Whew," Bill whistled loudly, wiping his brow as if to indicate that one was as close as it could get. "Had I missed that trailer, I think I'd of ended up on that highway, he scoffed.

Both Bill and Dave were soaking wet and shaking uncontrollably from the ice cold lake water, as they hurriedly strapped the boat in place, and finally drove up the ramp with the car heater blasting warm air on them.

Laughing at what was obviously a very close call, Bill starred at Dave while slowly reaching into his pocket. "Here is your damned GPS Float, now let's go and mark that aquifer so Ed can finally buy some property for us — you know our future just may depend on it," Bill whispered totally done in by what he'd just been through.

Bill had noticed an eagles nest in one of the taller Pine trees by the aquifer, and in less than ten miles they were pulling both cars off the road at the exact location the aquifer was dumping its pure spring water into Lake Superior.

"What a find!" Dave yelled, calling Ed on his cell phone to come and celebrate with them. As they made their way some two hundred yards to the shoreline, they both stood in awe as they watched the waves crashing against the huge granite rocks.

Thank God I didn't smash into those rocks, Bill thought to himself, realizing for the first time how dangerously close he'd come to doing just that, before he recklessly dipped the GPS float from the water.

"We'll have to wait until things calm down a bit before we can put on a wet suit and take some samples from the mouth of our aquifer," Dave said, obviously as anxious as Bill to see if a delta of gold had accumulated on the bottom of the lake.

"Dave, I can't believe we're standing here, maybe only a short distance away from what could be a treasure of insurmountable value," Bill chocked with tears running down his cheeks and still trembling uncontrollably from both the cold and the excitement.

"Well we can't do anything now," Dave said equally affected by the overwhelming feelings they were both experiencing. "So let's go wait in your warm car for Ed to get here."

As they waited they decided that Bill would make the first dive, as soon as the weather settled down, with the hope of bringing up a good sized sample of silt from the bottom.

"If we could build our Foundation on this spit of land, we could actually leave any treasure we find safely on the bottom of the lake, dredging only what we needed — and when and if we needed it," Dave said.

"I agree — in fact I bet we could install a suction dredge inside the basement of our foundation and extend a hose down into the lake. That way nobody would ever hear or see us sucking the silt from the bottom of the lake," Bill explained, "and we already have all the diving equipment we need.

"Yah, but we'll really do need to have Ed apply for a mineral mining permit, just to be on the safe side," Dave suggested just as Ed pulled up behind them, obviously anxious to ketch up on what was happening.

After they told Ed about Bill's frantic battle with those ten foot waves, and how this spit of land was a perfect place to build their foundation, Ed scowled, saying, "I hate to be the bearer of bad news but this is Cheyenne Reservation property, and I've already checked that out — and our chance of buying land here is zero.

"Are you serious?" Dave chuckled out loud. That's the best news yet. White Cloud has already offered us the right to build both the Clinic and the Kitcimanadoo Foundation on his reservation, and I'm almost certain he'd offer us a hundred year lease on this property if I'd ask him."

Ed's mouth dropped open, shouting, "You've gotta be kidding! And here I've been busting my butt searching for property for the last week!"

"Bill and I have to go back to White Cloud's home in the morning, and Ed, you need to come with us so you can get enough information to prepare the necessary lease or purchase papers, while Bill and I search out the location to drill their well, which is only a mile or so from the Chief's home. My God, when I think of it, we certainly haven't been running into too many problems lately, have we?" Dave whispered, raising both eyebrows and shaking his head to show his honest surprise at how well things were going.

The next morning, Ed and White Cloud met in the Chief's office to work out the terms of a long term lease for the property where they'd build both the Clinic and the Kitcimanadoo Foundation — while several tribe members helped set various electrodes at several locations near the path the monitor had traced the GPS float. Then after setting off the black powder charge the Electro-Seismic device eventually produced a computer report that pinpointed the best spot and depth to drill, even telling them what water yield they could expect. With that information, Dave called his well and water tower contractors and made final arrangements for them to take over here just as soon as they finished at Bear Claws Reservation.

Needless to say, White Cloud was very pleased and expressed his deep appreciative several times for everything

Dave and Bill were doing for his *Ojibwe Tribes*, definitely believing they were truly a gift from the Great Spirit Kitcimanadoo. "We will have a great celebration when we finish," the Chief said.

After Lake Superior at long last settled down, Bill awkwardly pulled on his thermal diving suit, not anticipating at all the freezing swim that was in store for him after he tested his air tanks and slipped into the calm mirror like surface of what was a raging sea just a few days ago. He was amazed at the clarity of the water as his eyes astonishingly scanned what looked like a very large sand bottom with only a small number of huge granite rocks protruding through the sand in a few areas. As he studied the mouth of the aquifer it proved to be at least ten feet wide and perhaps three to four feet high, and he could feel the current moving him out toward the open water where the depth steadily increased until it reached a sudden drop off maybe fifty yards from shore. As he swam towards the drop off the silt like sand rapidly changed to rock, suggesting that the silt like soil was fairly well contained in the area where the aquifer current could still be felt. Making his way back to the aquifer he swam along the bottom scoping large samples of soil into the bags he'd purposely brought with him for that purpose.

As Bill surfaced he removed his mask and said, "It doesn't look anything like the rest of the coastline we see up here. There's a sand beach as big as a football field down there, and I have a whole bag of that material for us to check out," he sputtered as water dripped off his mask and face. After taking a few breaths of fresh air, he continued, "That aquifer has to be dumping enormous amounts of spring water into the lake, In fact that current was strong enough to push me almost fifty yards out from shore, and all that silt like sand is a sight to see."

"Let's hope it's got some of the right stuff in it," Ed scoffed, not using the word gold intentionally as he quickly took Bill's bags of what looked like sand and dumped it into a pan and began swirling it in some lake water to see if there were any gold flecks settling to the bottom — and within moments they all stared in awe at almost all of the material clinging to the ridges in the pan.

"My God," Dave yelled, "This has to be almost pure," and then he stopped and chocked out, "mineral."

As they stood there staring at each other, aghast at what they were looking at, it finally dawned on them that the football field of silt deposit was possibly the Mother Lode of Mother Lodes, a find that had to be worth billions.

"We have to find a quite place where we can talk confidentially," Dave said, "Or this whole thing could really get out of hand very fast."

"And I better get that mining permit figured out fast, and I'm not yet sure of everything that's involved there," Ed added.

After Bill changed clothes they stopped briefly at the motel to check out, and then Dave and Bill returned Chief White Clouds Car, while Ed returned his rental vehicle before they headed back to the Twin Cities — agreeing to confidentially discuss everything and anything on the way home.

Chapter 17

How Did The Too Big To Fail
Investment Banks Get So Powerful?

David Rockefeller, once the powerful head of the Chase Manhattan Bank, now the retail and service arm of JP Morgan Chase, created the Tri Lateral Commission (TC), which included international financiers, industrialists, media magnates, union bosses, academics and former political figures who soon became very influential in advising, consulting, and taking over our elected politicians responsibilities. Later, as the TC gained greater control the TBTF banks influenced almost all members of Congress through their sizable donations, while keeping today's totally dysfunctional and ridiculous two party systems in perpetual conflict. Then in 1998, several of these same powerful leaders proposed to take down the Glass-Steagall Act of 1933, which had protected the people's savings for some seventy years following the Great Depression. They intended to accomplish this through a proposed merger between Citycorp, a commercial bank holding company, and Travelers Group, an insurance company. This merger was clearly a violation of the Glass–Steagall Act, yet their privately owned Federal Reserve debatably issued a temporary waiver. Than a year later, the implementation of this merger played a key role in the accomplishment of their plan, with the advance assurances from the following key players: Allen Greenspan of the Federal

*Reserve; John Reed, former Citycorp Chairman and head of their Commercial banking system; Sandy Wile, then the head of Citicorp's investment banking division; Phil Gramm, a Republican U.S. Senator, who under a stressful situation resigned from the Senate to become Vice President of the UBS; Robert Rubin the former Secretary of the Treasure under Bill Clinton and now a current board member of this new company called Citigroup; The Chairman of both the Senate and House Banking Commissions; and Bill Clinton, President, who agreed to take down the Glass- Steagall Act and sign into law this new Gramm — Leach — Bliley Act. This new act repealed very significant parts of the Glass- Steagall Act of 1933, removing through deregulation all previous barriers in the market among banking companies, securities companies and insurance companies, which once prohibited any one institution from acting in any combination of an investment bank, a commercial bank, or an insurance company. At that time, in 1999, the United States had a 230 billion positive budget, and had paid off 360 billion in bad debts from 1998 to 1999 — so things were looking good for the first time in years. But by opening the door so banks could regulate themselves in 1998, and then in 2001 and 2003 by providing sizable tax cuts to the wealthy business owners while **We the People** were assured that the public would indirectly benefit through trickledown economics. What the U.S. found however, was that greed overshadowed any form of public benefit and since the 1933 Glass – Steagall Act was no longer there to protect the tax payer or the banks, things rapidly began to collapse. The indiscriminate selling of subprime under insured mortgages for quick profit, not only left the client in jeopardy but the banks, insurance, and investors were all eventually left with valueless holdings that could unmistakably take down the entire banking industry. Clearly this demonstrated the* *inability for banks to regulate themselves. The first sign of trouble was when two Bear Stearns hedge funds threatened collapse in July 2007, and because Bear had less than adequate insurance to protect against their losses, the Federal Reserve Chairman Ben Bernanke, Tim Geithner, then president of the Federal Reserve Bank of New York, and Treasury Secretary Hank Paulson and other government officials urgently met to discuss Bear's precarious position and what a Bear bankruptcy could mean for the broader markets. Fearing a total international melt down, the Fed Board members authorized an emergency loan to the troubled investment bank, to be provided through the J.P. Morgan-Stanley investment bank which was in turn required to acquire Bear Stearns with fed money. The Lehman investment bank was next to collapse but this time the Fed decided to let them fail, which ignited the catastrophic international banking failures of 2008. Fannie Mae, Freddie Mac and American International Group Inc. (AIG) an International Insurance Company were all waiting in the wings to fail, and to prevent a total collapse the U.S. Government, the Feds injected an 85 billion dollar loan into AIG, which they felt was too big to let fail and could have devastating effect on the world market. However, this time the U.S. government acquired a 79.9% equity stake in AIG. Then on October 3rd, 2008, as the financial crisis grew, a locked door meeting brought together the "TBTF" banks and Ben Bernanke and Hank Paulson to consummate the 700 billion dollar Troubled Asset Relief Program (TARP) bailout, where the Federal Reserve disbursed $601,447,107,758 billion dollars to 928 recipients. Six of the "TBTF" were required to accept some 460 billion in loans with Morgan Stanley receiving 107 billion; Bank of America 91.4 billion and Citigroup 99.5 billion. Coupled closely with this bailout were Fannie Mae who received 116 billion, Freddie Mac 71 billion*

*and then later under the Obama administration GM received a
57 billion dollar loan. Isn't it ridiculous that these plutocrats
can get Bernanke to issue over 600 billion to some 928 profit
earning recipients and yet we can't bail out Social Security or
our healthcare services?*

*Yes, it was the greed of these international "TBTF"
investment banks and corporations that opened the door to
today's worldwide financial crisis. In fact this same Oligarchy
has now deregulated international trade, Wall Street, the
housing mortgage and banking standards which placed over
eleven million homes under water, as well as promoted the
blatant theft of customer money from MF Global — and now
more recently failed to even report foreign bank loans of 1.2
trillion. And yes, they've now successfully changed our once
powerful Democracy to that of a lesser nation that can be far
more readily controlled under what has been clearly trending
toward a Puppet Government. Isn't it strange that every time
we try to shrink their "TBTF" banks their amoral self-interests
and big money overpowers our totally dysfunctional
Washington clique that we always thought represented **We the
People** of this once highly respected Republic? As a result, our
politicians known as the enablers or plutocrats are standing
with dirt on their hands, too frightened to acknowledge their
part in accepting the benefits and the easy money they've
obtained for the political favors these profit corporations have
received. And so our nation is caught in a credibility gap that
stifles both our recovery and reform, and there does not seem
to be the ability or the will to return to our previous healthy
market in this once great nation — or even a balanced
economy. In fact, this type of power struggle detests any type
of free market that involves fairness and transparency as they
aggressively seek to deregulate, decentralize and control the
rules and regulations that fair and open competition requires.*

Why is this? Because ethical competition provides a serious hindrance over the control of this Oligarchy's huge profits and creates too much uncertainty and risk for their monopolies. But this is why all wealthy Aristocracies intentionally employ deregulation and decentralization — while their wealth is used to assure one of total control and dominance through monopoly. And this is why this very wealthy enclave of International Investment Bankers also seeks to openly control the United States Armed Forces and the World Market through a NWO that can better take the risk out of their equation. And you know what? It's not as if we were never previously informed, for this is exactly what President Eisenhower once warned us about. Under this type of fascistic control they use their own books and standards without having to deal with the same standards our small businessmen have to deal with. It's very much like our politicians have their own government benefits and healthcare and retirement programs because they are allowed to set their own standards, while our government benefits are considered socialistic in nature. Typically, far too many politicians foster this culture of the very wealthy having their own standards and benefits of hypocrisy and cheating without restraint; a predatory class of world entrepreneurs and politicians without allegiance to anyone but their own greed and hunger for money, power and control. Therefore, it becomes a simple matter for the very wealthy, by this private fraud tactic, to constantly steal from this Government of the People under their set of rules. And this is how these international bankers became so powerful.

As they drove toward the Twin Cities Ed spoke first, saying, "If you guys had any doubt about me, I'm sure in this thing for the long haul, and I'm now more than willing to serve as the Foundation's Executive Secretary — but I have a lot of things I'd like to accomplish with all this new found wealth, and I don't want to see us repeat the same mistakes I'm watching happen in our country right now. So I feel you guys really need to know where I'm coming from."

"My feelings are very much the same," Bill added, "and I think we should use this travel time to speak out on what we all really think this Foundation should look like in the future. That's before we go off half cocked and mess things up."

"We don't have a better time to do this than right now." Dave added, "Why don't you start Ed, and when we're all done talking we'll see if we can find common ground to do something meaningful with this potential fortune were sitting on."

"Alright, if I can get you two to sit back and listen, perhaps I can tell you why I'm interested in Banks and what I think we could do to change today's political scene." With that, Ed paused just long enough to adjust his position so he was a little more comfortable.

"Each of you has read that brochure I picked up in Duluth, and I agree totally with what it said about the ***Too Big To Fail Banks***. Commercial Banks use to be the only type of bank that existed until these damned International Investment Bankers took over and brought profit into what was once a secure system for the everyday citizen that only wanted to protect their savings and their mortgage. But now that Wall Street has taken over, so their banks can make these huge profits, we've lost our once secure banking system that previously functioned within clearly defined ethical standards — and now with these investment risks, we're all paying for the loses these banks incur when they take risks with our hard earned savings and mortgage money. I think our Foundation could help regular middle class Americans start a whole new group of nonprofit commercial savings banks by helping a few middle class people buy up some of our failing small commercial banks that could receive loans from us at a very low one percent interest rate — later paying back these loans as they help us reestablish smaller controllable high quality banks with standards that protect the middle class," Ed stopped to think a moment and change his thought.

"You've all heard how these Wall Street control freaks claim that any public service to the people in a Democracy is Socialism — just like a socialistic government controlled by powerful rulers of an Aristocracy; an Empire; a Monarchy; a Kingdom; a Realm; or even a Domain; when we really should be scared stiff of the Wall Street privately owned Federal Reserve and these ***Too Big To Fail Banks*** that are controlling almost all of today's international wealth. These wealthy bankers and international corporate leaders are the same guys that anxiously sought Fascism, Socialism, or Communism in 1944 — just so it would give them greater control over their wealth. Hell, a few social programs that protect the middle class's benefits and services to humanity are no more socialistic than the current Sun City Retirement communities that are forming all over our country. So that's why I'd like us to start a chain of small controllable nonprofit banks that compete head on with these big boys, providing these small bankers one percent loans to get started so they can once again provide the middle class secure savings and mortgages at a reasonable fixed rate the public can afford. I also think these nonprofit banks could in turn help many more small businesses to get started so they could compete cost effectively for Government contracts — thereby potentially improving our infrastructure in this country, which is currently going to hell in a hand basket. If you've ever studied what's really going on in today's world, you'll find these wealthy international profit seeking bankers control or own almost all the international corporations as well as our government loans and the Federal Reserve — and now they've even bought off the entire Senate and the House of Representatives so they've become totally dysfunctional. And damn it, it's about time we the people wake up and do something about this. And I mean now. We've also got to stop all these political donations immediately and I have some ideas on that which I'll share with you later." With this Ed sat back and took a deep breath, "So that's what I'd like to do as your Executive Director."

"What are your ideas on stopping those political donations?" Dave asked.

"I want to survey the entire nation on whether they'd like to amend the Constitution, and stop all these corrupting political donations by forcing our politicians to live within in their salary instead of all becoming instant millionaires through today's ridiculous Wall Street buy off. I feel the entire nation is crying for this to happen, but they have no voice in the matter, so I'd like to help give them a voice."

"Wow, I'm for that," Bill said, "And I've also got some ideas about what we could do with our healthcare system we're watching collapse right before our eyes. That's if you're finished Ed?"

"Yah, go ahead, I could talk for ever, and I probably will if you don't take over and give us your two cents worth."

"Okay, let me add to what you've already said so eloquently." Bill said, pulling over to the side of the road to let Ed drive.

"I have a lot to say, and I can better tell you my thoughts without running off the road if I sit here in the back seat," Bill chuckled as he shut the back seat door.

"First of all let me say that I think I could capably manage our new healthcare clinic once it's built, and I've been leaning toward healthcare administration for a long time, instead of practicing medicine. I'd also like to get some of White Cloud's tribe members into some training programs right away so we'd be able to eventually staff this new facility with well trained tribe members."

With that Bill shifted his position to get more comfortable.

"Back in 1913, the Flexner report first helped to establish healthcare standards and regulations that were previously nonexistent, and now these standards are once again disappearing in light of Wall Street's deregulation Ed speaks of. Why? — Because of their endless appetite for profits. And probably you don't even remembers how healthcare administrators once met with community leaders to implement Cost Containment Programs and Regional Healthcare Planning — or the 1919 Hospitalization Act and the 1944 Hill Burton Hospital Survey and Construction Act that helped build over eighty percent of this nation's hospital beds under one percent federal loans so our healthcare services could help take care of this nations wounded and disabled veterans of World War I and II. And you also need to know that back then we were once ranked number one in healthcare in the world by the World Health Organization, instead of 37th today." As Bill tried to relax, he felt the tension rising in his neck and back, just as it always did when he talked about healthcare in the United States.

"Then more recently, in 1945, these entrepreneurial politicians passed the McCarran Fergusson Act, which sought to create profits from what was once a very successful nonprofit privately owned single prepayment human service for the sick and disabled of this country. Yes, that's true, prior to this Act we previously had a very successful nonprofit healthcare insurance program for the middle class, which was equally available to all citizens of the United States under a single community prepayment system that was entirely privately owned and managed. But now this new McCarran Fergusson Act opened the door to a very aggressive profit insurance take-over that began in 1965, where profit-oriented insurance was suddenly given an open door to function without regulation at either the federal or state level, and as a result we could no longer protect our once very successful community rated nonprofit prepayment plan. This new profit insurance marketing program persuaded healthy younger clients to buy cheaper low-risk Group tiered insurance policies in a process termed *Bait and Switch*. They did this by selling "Group" rating the same as "Community" rating.

"What's "Community" rating?" Dave asked.

"That's where everyone paid the same rate," Bill replied. "Of course the gullible public quickly sought the slightly cheaper group insurance rate, not understanding that each group rate would eventually increase as its members inevitably required increased healthcare services. As a result, the nonprofit system was increasingly forced to cover more and more patients with health problems, which the profit-oriented insurance companies intentionally dumped by increasing the sicker patient's premiums to unrealistic levels. The clients that had previously jumped ship from our once very successful nonprofit community system were later stunned when they eventually became undesirable members of what soon became known as the "Death Spiral." In insurance jargon, the Death Spiral describes the results of group pool rating where profit insurance sells a policy for a year or two, creating a pool of policy holders — and then after a while, this group is closed, and from that point forward no new clients are allowed to come into that pool. Profit insurance would then sell the next group pool in a process called "Tiering" and as those in the older pool slowly aged, the number and size of their insurance claims inevitably increased, and that's when group rating allowed the profit oriented insurance company to jack up that individual pool's rates. Healthy clients could leave a pool to get lower rates, but older clients, women of child-bearing age, and those in poor health couldn't obtain a new policy to cover what they termed preexisting health problems, and eventually the premiums in these group pools were raised so high that almost all the patients that couldn't qualify for other insurance were forced to quit and become members of the increasing number of un-insured. In other words, they entered the Death Spiral!"

"You've gotta be kidding," Dave said.

"I wish I were, but that's the honest to God truth." Bill said.

"Prior to all this profit insurance," Bill continued, "only four percent of the average per-capita's annual income was required to purchase high quality nonprofit community insurance; while today we spend minimally twenty percent and often far more when a family encounters a serious healthcare problem. On top of all this, we're taxed for some twenty Federal programs including a very special and costly healthcare benefit provided to our politicians, who on the other hand state they do not want to provide government coverage for **We the People**. They want to give us a five to eight thousand dollar certificate from our own tax dollar to buy our own insurance. As a result of the McCarran Fergusson Act, President Johnson was forced to start Medicare, for those who were unable to afford the current costly profit oriented group healthcare insurance, thereby further lowering the bad debts for the hundreds of unmanageable profit seeking insurance companies that have now essentially decentralized and deregulated almost all of our overall standards and cost accounting in today's healthcare system."

With this Bill paused to gather his thoughts.

"As a result, our healthcare costs continued to spiral out of control as these politicians decentralize and deregulate this country's once very successful nonprofit single payer human service for the sick and disabled into a confused out of control Government subsidized and profit seeking two level system — one for the wealthy, and one for the poor — and remember this is in a country that still professes to be a Democracy. What I want to do, just like Ed is start a small single nonprofit health insurance company so they can compete head on with the profits at a much lower cost to the patient. I'd also like to team up with a few selected nonprofit hospitals that are willing to restructure into a cost accounting systems and go back to a total nonprofit system that serves as a benefit to the middle class. Hopefully we could eventually return to a total single nonprofit system that could cut out all profit insurance, and then we could maybe have some clout when we were large enough to negotiate fair prices for all pharmaceuticals, and hopefully stop all political kickbacks.

The thing that both Ed and I agree on is these profit seekers have invaded the areas that have provided human service benefits to this nation's middle class for years, the workers that do all the work in this country, and they are the ones who should have their benefits protected from these wealthy profit seeking entrepreneurs. As Ed put it so nicely, that's not socialism, its protecting our public service benefits to our workers, the backbone of this great Republic we call a Democracy."

"My God, how am I going to follow all this," Dave said without hesitation. "What you guys have said is amazing — I couldn't have two more qualified partners if I searched for the rest of my life. All I really want to do is help out Bear Claw and White Cloud, and based on what I've seen happen to them, I think we should all start worrying much more about what we're doing to our environment. If we don't — future generations will bear the consequences of our dysfunctional politician's failure to even attempt to meet this country's carbon reduction requirements and the growing carbon emissions in our atmosphere. And because of this we're seeing all kinds of warnings, like weather extremes and climate changes, temperature increases, and far more floods and storms. We also know our water shortages are becoming extremely critical and yet Washington does nothing about it." With that Dave paused a moment to gather his thoughts.

"And Ed, as your Duluth article said — with today's exponentially growing population of seven billion human beings we're becoming seriously out of balance with the finite number of global resources this planet can ever provide. They projected that our global population would reach 13 billion by 2075, and 26 billion in 2145, which is well beyond the earth's capability to support, which they said will never happen since humanity will have ceased well before that unless we find another planet to over-populate. Doesn't that scare the hell out of you?" Dave asked, shrugging his shoulders in disbelief.

"So I've also got several suggestions I'd like to accomplish. Lately I've been thinking that we should get a permit to dredge up all that Taconite Tailings they dumped in Lake Superior, which nobody seems to want to be responsible for. In our request for a mining permit we could also ask that we be allowed to process any valuable minerals we find along the north shore of Lake Superior and never even mention the word gold. And since we're only going to process gold as we need it, we won't be declaring that much every year anyway. And on the surface, we'd really be doing them a big favor by also removing the tailings. And since our roads are all going to hell across the entire United States, why don't we mix the wet tailings we suck up with Canadian sand oil, and use it to resurface the roads across America."

Dave paused to let them digest that idea before continuing

"Since you guys also think we should help the middle class start businesses with loans at one percent, let's get a few Indians to start the dredge and road surfacing companies in Minnesota, and then expand more companies all across the country if it catches on. That way we can help to stop the bigger companies from playing these ridiculous money kick-back games with our Congress."

"That's a hell of a good idea," Bill interrupted, as Ed looked over his shoulder at Bill and nodded in agreement.

"And since we now have all this unbelievable equipment that can find deep spring water, why don't we ask Mior to start a water seeking company that can dig wells that aren't contaminated by pesticides and fertilizers, and help solve our water shortage and water contamination crisis in this country. Yes, it's all very clear to me that our politicians don't ever want to see a Master Plan for water or our environment in this once respected and advanced nation. In fact, our well digger told me water usage has tripled since 1960, with the current demand for freshwater already requiring more than 64 billion cubic meters a year. He told me that by 2030 it is estimated that some 3.9 billion people will be living under severe water stress, and our agriculture and animal and plant life are already being threatened, while adequate soil for plant growth has also been trending in the wrong direction. He told me melting glaciers and ice caps are seriously depleting so much of our fresh water that it is becoming even more worrisome than the energy crisis and that many of our lakes and rivers are already drying up. As glacier water turns into salt water, he believes our shorelines will in the not too distant future be covered by as much as eight feet of sea water, reducing even further the amount of land for our ever growing population." With that Dave again paused for a moment.

"Bill, I bet you're well aware that there are all kinds of studies that are showing serious statistical links with water contaminants and neurological diseases, which are estimated to increase to one in every three people over the next 20 years. We already know that residents who consume private well water and live within 500 feet of farmland where pesticide are used are almost twice as likely to acquire some type of neurological disorder. Paraquat was banned by the European countries, but not in United States, and the widespread use of pesticides and weed killers such as Bromacil, Diuron, Simazine, and Atrzine have all been banned in Europe while they are still the most widely used herbicides in the United States. Why? Because our politicians don't want to put a damper on those huge kickbacks and profits the corporations provide them. Sure we know which chemicals are the culprits, but what's the government doing about it — nothing! So currently we have no transition away from water like there may be from fossil fuels, such as wind, solar or other energy sources — but we can't replace water. And we can't forget that water also has an enormous impact on food and soil irrigation. I think the most important thing we have to say in our Corporate By-Laws is that the three of us don't want to take all this wealth and protect it for ourselves as these powerful International Bankers and Corporations have done,"

With that Ed sharply interrupted Dave. "I sure agree, in fact when someone applies for a grant, our By-Laws should force us to apply the concepts we just discussed here before we can authorize the use of any foundation's money."

"If we take adequate salaries and benefits so we aren't starving to death, there should be no problem as I see it," Bill responded. "Dave, what do you think?"

"I agree whole heartedly. If we can stick to our mission being *to benefit the working middle class,* maybe we can change some things in this crazy profit seeking country we live in."

"And if they think that's being socialistic, that's the type of giving I'm all for," Ed added. "I've had enough of their fascist control that's destroying this country we all once respected, as well as every other nation in the world did."

"One more thing I'd like to say," Dave added. "Since the United States and the rest of the world all find themselves in a sustainability crisis that will inevitably destroy the ecological balance of humankind if mankind doesn't act soon, our foundation should and must urgently take steps to correct this, and that should be spelled out in our written Mission Statement. In fact I believe we might even eventually legally challenge these powerful plutocrats that represent us and are intentionally ignoring our global environment with complete disregard for our air quality and climate; the misuse of our environmental energy, water and the food chain; our population crisis; and the open deregulating and decentralizing of our transportation, education, retirement and healthcare systems. They also need to understand that we are well past World Peak Oil and that exploring for oil is no longer the solution with nine out of ten wells ending up dry holes, while perhaps only one in a hundred wells ever becoming a significant find. They know full well that drilling deeper than 15,000 feet is not the answer since 7,000 to15, 000 feet is where oil is found in what's called the oil window, where the organic-rich soil sediments are hot enough to change into oil molecules — while drilling deeper, like 15,000 feet, the oil becomes so hot that the oil molecules are changed into natural gas. And every one of them have been told that if we started today we could still not produce significant oil within ten years, which falls well after the shortage we're already experiencing. Yet they've done nothing about it, and we need to someday hold them accountable, because they knew we have no renewable combination of energy sources that can replace the energy we get from oil. In fact, all our current renewable energy combined cannot even begin to produce even a small fraction of today's industrial or technological energy required. And worse yet, if we continue to remain insensitive to this looming disaster, our debt-based economy that depends on economic growth to survive will soon be gasping for air because this finite global resource is some day going to run out. In fact we've allowed our current carbon emissions and air pollution to result in a rise in carbon emissions to a level of 390 parts per million globally, as compared to 280 parts per million prior to the start of our industrial revolution." With that Dave took a deep breath. "So I really I think we need to take some type of legal action against these powerful plutocrats so they will never do this again.

"Yes, you're absolutely right," Ed said, "and I also have a plan of how we can perhaps change the Constitution, so we can get these dysfunctional two party politicians that are in eternal conflict out of office — maybe permanently. It may not work, but we can at least give it a try, and although I can't give you the details today, I promise I'll prepare and present it to you guys in the very near future."

"That sounds interesting," Bill said, "and now I think we should bring things to a close for now, by saying that when our appointed representatives seek profits from human services such as Health Care, or the very infrastructure that protects our environment and our natural resources that are essential to support life, they are destroying the middle class's earned benefits that have always previously been sheltered under some type of tax program or nonprofit system in this once very successful Republic of the People. Very much like the members of Congress and the U.S. Senate vigorously protect their own socialistic government type healthcare insurance and retirement program they secretly and totally control for their own benefit.

The next morning Ed completed the mining application for the entire north shore of Lake Superior along the Arrowhead Country, so their Foundation could not only attempt to recover the dangerous tailings that had been dumped in the lake, but also some minerals — while Bill and Dave met with their attorney to finalize the Kitchimanadoo Foundation's By-Laws and Mission Statement after meeting with their assayer to confirm the highest quality of gold they'd just found on their brief venture to the remote aquifer on the north shore of Lake Superior. They also worked out their plan for reclaiming gold bars and paying tax on minerals and other earnings under their new nonprofit company that involved the complex accounting and issuance of grants and loans that could be paid back at one percent interest. The following three days were spent with the architect Ed hired, discussing the clinic and foundation buildings, the parking facilities and the special dredging accommodations they needed. They decided the water for both buildings could be obtained through their own aquifer and drilling company managed by Mior — and their sewage system would initially require a septic system, with long range plans being made for a far more comprehensive sewage system that could handle the entire reservation.

Their Mission Statement dealt primarily with the improvement of air quality and climate; the proper use of environmental energy, the water and the food chain; the resolution of the population crisis under a nonprofit structure that protects the middle class, the backbone of this nation work force, as well as their earned benefits that have always previously been sheltered under some type of tax program or nonprofit system in this Government of the People. And as Ed had indicated, the eventual modification of this country's Constitution so we the people could eventually get these dysfunctional and corrupt politicians out of our Government system, which is a government of the people – not just a big government we need to downsize.

Epilogue

Six months after making application for a mining permit the Kitchimanadoo Foundation received approval and purchased a used dredge and barge, a tug boat, and three trucks from the out of business Reserve Mining Company that built the original taconite processing plant at Silver Bay and dumped the tailings into Lake Superior in the late 1950's. All the Indians that once worked for them lost their jobs when they closed, but many were now employed by this new dredging company mixing the water soaked tailings with Canadian sand oil, which they stored on their Cheyenne Reservation. This new business was owned by the Indians and they sold this approved asphalt type road surfacing product as an effective road cover that not only repaired our nation's roads cost effectively, but helped to reduce slippery road surfaces during the winter months.

Both reservation water towers were also completed and operational under the new Mior Management Company, and Mior was being kept very busy finding new pure water sources throughout Minnesota, Wisconsin and Iowa. His new company used the new Electro-Seismic Technology to find clean groundwater by setting off a powder charge that sent a sound pressure wave 1500 feet deep from four electrodes placed in the ground, which were hooked up to a computer — rather than using water witching willows.

The land lease for the Clinic and the Foundation was also in place well before any construction started and now, some sixteen months later, the contractor was putting the finishing touches to the new facilities that Dave, Bill and Ed were anxiously waiting to occupy. In the basement, on the lake side of the building, a dredge pump system was in place and had already been tested, sucking ample amounts of minerals without anyone even noticing. As more money was needed, Bill manually directed the long hose to various locations in the huge field of valuable minerals for processing. The Foundation's Mission Statement also promised to try and stop the **Political Stress Syndrome** that American's were feeling and the terrible stranglehold the TBTF banks had on this great nation. More importantly, they would soon try to stop the donations to our Congress and Senate, as they methodically tried to acquire small banks and hopefully someday replace this nation's dependence on the international TBTF system that owned our country's Federal Reserve.

As promised, Ed outlined his strategy for appropriately amending the Constitution of the United States through first surveying every voting citizen of the United States, by mailing some 209,279,149 questionnaires that were already under computer analysis. The following is a sample of the survey:

Note: Please complete the attached proposed policy and Constitutional Amendments Survey and mail in the attached prepaid envelope, where it will be analyzed by an unbiased Ad Hoc Constitutional Committee of the people of the United State, and the results will then be aired nationally:

1. *Under the highest priority we should demand the Senate and Congress immediately prepare credible U.S Master Plans for:* •*Population Growth;* • *Advance alternative energy and natural resource conservation;* • *The return of our healthcare to a nonprofit prepayment Health Care*

system under a single private and /or government system; • *Implement Environmental changes that protect the quality and quantity of our   air, water and food;* • *Provide adequate government support for this nation's Infrastructure, Transportation, Education, and Law enforcement.*

YES ☐   NO ☐   I DON'T KNOW ☐

2. *Repeal the Federal Reserve Act and the IRS code, with the U.S. taking back the Federal Reserve and its banks.*

YES ☐   NO ☐   I DON'T KNOW ☐

3. *Reinstate the Steagall Act of 1933, which prohibits any one institution from acting in any combination of an investment bank, a commercial bank, or an insurance company.*

YES ☐   NO ☐   I DON'T KNOW ☐

4. *Reinstate the gold standard and balance the budget with auditable internal fiscal control under a government owned Federal Bank System.*

YES ☐   NO ☐   I DON'T KNOW ☐

5. *The United States shall routinely audit, report, validate and control all "capital" and "current" federal expenditures and capital improvements.*

YES ☐   NO ☐   I DON'T KNOW ☐

6. *The United States shall enforce earmark transparency under open public scrutiny.*

    YES ☐   NO ☐   I DON'T KNOW ☐

7. *The United States Treasury shall be responsible for the creation of all interest-free and debt-free money and establish a solid pay as you go standard that aggressively repays all current loans without borrowing the money.*

    YES ☐   NO ☐   I DON'T KNOW ☐

8. *Make it unlawful for politicians to accept any donations of money, gifts or financial benefits during or after their tenure in office. Reasonable Federal financial assistance should be made available to qualified candidates running for political office. All politicians shall be provided the same Health Care and Social Security Benefits available to all citizens, thereby discontinuing the politician's current healthcare and retirement benefits.*

    YES ☐   NO ☐   I DON'T KNOW ☐

9. *Tax all citizens and corporations equally and adequately, including off shore corporations for goods sold either within or to the United States.*

    YES ☐   NO ☐   I DON'T KNOW ☐

10. *No more U.S participation in wars unless this nation is attacked and all international terrorist threats and wars shall be suppressed through the United Nation's.*

      YES ☐   NO ☐   I DON'T KNOW ☐

11. *Establish a more modest U.S. presence in the world.*

      YES ☐   NO ☐   I DON'T KNOW ☐

12. *The United States should immediately eliminate the dysfunctional and costly duplicative two party system, allowing states to have a stronger single voice in setting federal standards, thereby eliminating the current extreme liberal or conservative partisan conflicts at a substantially reduced cost to the tax payer.*

      YES ☐   NO ☐   I DON'T KNOW ☐

13. *Immediately reduce the Pentagon budget by half.*

      YES ☐   NO ☐   I DON'T KNOW ☐

14. *Expand current and new U.S. business opportunities promoting locally made and grown products under a competitive business profile that enhances future U.S. free market profit potentials, while reducing international off shore corporate monopolies.*

      YES ☐   NO ☐   I DON'T KNOW ☐

15. *Implement nonprofit status for all approved services and benefits to humankind under centralized and efficiently managed standards and regulations.*

     YES □   NO □   I DON'T KNOW □

16. *Set standards for a president's job description, requiring he or she complete a Master Plan describing their written goals and objectives they intend to accomplish while in office. The candidate's Master Plan shall then be made available to the public prior to election and each candidate must sign an agreement that they understand they are to represent, and provide bipartisan leadership to the people of this nation and that they are vested with the responsibility of representing and protecting this nation's working class, their human services, and their open and free market. Every candidate shall meet pre- established educational and leadership requirements, principles and responsibilities, and the government should conduct an unbiased psychological evaluation before placing any candidate up for election*

     YES □   NO □   I DON'T KNOW □

17. *All Federal and State Contracts shall universally utilize competitive bidding principles and all members of the Congress shall be restricted from either granting or influencing no-bid contracts to favored corporations.*

     YES □   NO □   I DON'T KNOW □

18. *All public business and policy shall be open to public scrutiny.*

    YES ☐   NO ☐   I DON'T KNOW ☐

19. *All tax-exempt foundations that serve as repositories for divested interests, making their assets non-taxable to avoid estate and gift taxes shall be brought to an end.*

    YES ☐   NO ☐   I DON'T KNOW ☐

20. *Balance all trade deficits and tax all foreign trade equally.*

    YES ☐   NO ☐   I DON'T KNOW ☐

21. *Voting systems shall become auditable, and be based on the populous vote.*

    YES ☐   NO ☐   I DON'T KNOW ☐

22. *Stop policing, colonizing and controlling other countries natural resources, and close all international military bases.*

    YES ☐   NO ☐   I DON'T KNOW ☐

23. *Re-instate the executive order banning assassinations by any US government agency*

    YES ☐   NO ☐   I DON'T KNOW ☐

24. *The United States must stop exporting and importing jobs under today's New World Government strategy, protecting this country's sovereignty while discouraging any type of New World Order, or any international industrial monopoly. Globalization of the open market and the encouragement of human nonprofit services to humankind shall be diligently promoted.*

YES ☐ NO ☐ I DON'T KNOW ☐

Please attach your additional proposals on a separate page.

Signature:_____ Address:_____

Since the survey was already receiving an overwhelming response and the preliminary results were predominantly "yes" answers, Ed was gathering enough ammunition to either have the results voted on nationally, or placed before the Congress and the Senate for an open vote that would expose the plutocrats. If the recommendations were not approved by the politicians the unbiased Ad Hoc Constitutional Committee planned to take it to the President, demanding the proposed recommendations be brought before the entire nation for a vote.

Ed had also helped the owners of some nineteen failing banks, under his loan program, to become nonprofit banks that functioned under the former Steagall Act of 1933 standards, and as a result were required to issue mortgages that would provide the middle class secure savings and mortgages at a reasonable fixed rate the public could afford. These banks also were required to help small businesses get started so they could contract cost effectively for Government contracts that improved the overall infrastructure of this country,

Bill had enrolled some fifteen women and men from the reservation into the University of Minnesota, to prepare for careers in healthcare and eventually take care of their own tribe members when the clinic eventually became operational. He'd also applied for State licensure and entered into contracts with both St. Luke's and St. Joseph's hospitals in Duluth under the Foundation's own single nonprofit prepayment insurance plan, which was a community supplemental plan where all patients received equal health care and paid equally. Hopefully the plan would eventually replace profit insurance and Medicare was excited by the potential, already agreeing to bid pharmaceuticals competitively with the foundation's plan.

As Dave had proposed, he was actively challenging many of these powerful plutocrats legally for intentionally ignoring our global environment with complete disregard for our air quality and climate; the misuse of our environmental energy, water and food chain; our population crisis; and the open deregulating and decentralizing of our transportation, education and our retirement and healthcare systems. His legal lobbyists were also meeting daily with many Congressional and Senate members who were on the take, scaring the hell out of them as he secretly audited their financial dealings with their PACs and Super PACs with an intensity that had never before been seen in Washington.

And the Kitchimanadoo Foundation was only beginning.

Isn't it amazing what money can't do when it isn't totally controlled by a wealthy International Oligarchy or a corrupt group of Plutocrats, which currently comprises the nemesis of our Democracy?